what lies IN THE understory

E.C. MAENPAA

WHAT LIES IN THE UNDERSTORY

Cover & Layout
Michelle Fairbanks, Fresh Design

ISBN Print 978-1-7389319-0-3

What Lies in the Understory is a work of fiction.
The opinions expressed are those of the characters and should not be confused with the author's. Names, characters, places, and incidents are either the product of the author's imagination or are used fictitiously. Any resemblance to actual events or persons, living or dead, is entirely coincidental. Some locations are, however, very real and spectacular.

Dedication

To my husband Steve, my partner for life, a wonderful father and a great cook. Thank-you for supporting me to do what I love and thank-you for raising good men.

Preface

The act of writing fiction is born from the art of imagination. While this story is a work of fiction, the excerpts you are about to read from the prologue and the main character's perspective are derived from both my imagination and my memory of the story of the Wild Woman of the Woods, a supernatural being. There are variations of this story from different cultures around the world, and my personal experience with it is drawn from childhood years spent living in Kwakwa̱ka̱'wakw territory, along the northeastern shores of Vancouver Island. I recognize that in order to weave pieces of reality into this fictional story, it required me to pay careful attention to respectful use of language. It also required me to take the time to reach out for consultation, do the research and make careful considerations. This is part of my reconciliation journey. It would never be my intent to be disrespectful of culture or to appropriate culture. I humbly acknowledge my work and my learning as a guest on these shared ancestral lands.

The story of the Wild Woman made a significant impact on me. She terrified me as a child, and was an effective deterrent against mischievous behaviour and forbidden wandering in the forest near dusk. She might capture you and eat you up! I have carried her in my mind for many years and have recently learned that she is not just a threatening figure, she is also an enormous force of strength. One who can bring protection and revival. She encompasses the spirit of the forest and ancient feminine knowledge. My hope is that I've done her justice in this work of fiction and that you find her in the forest too some day. In a good way, of course.

Life is not easy for any of us.

But what of that?

We must have perseverance and above all,
confidence in ourselves.

We must believe we are gifted for something

and that this thing must be attained.

~ Marie Curie

Prologue

She moves slowly, with a heavy presence, cutting through the thick fog that lingers between the cedars. Darkness had started to creep in and with it, her breath growing louder. Pangs of hunger bring her to huff and grunt between steps, over the heavy blankets of vibrant, green moss. Always hungry, though it was desperate now.

Oh to have the good fortune to happen upon a child who runs amongst the trees, who does not heed the warning.

Before the darkness comes, she hears them scattering from the trails that make their breath smell sweet with salmonberries. She silently wails. Her black, wiry hair is electrified with the excitement of execution. Her thoughts bemoan the emptiness.

To find a child who defies the rule.

She longs to flash her red hot eyes into theirs. They will look at her with wide, liquid pools of terrified awe before she takes them. Her hunger turns over with protest in her vast stomach.

She heaves her heavy body over the stumps, taking in the air, thick with the heady scent of sweet, young skin.

She could hear the careful footsteps of two young children moving through the trees that day. The late afternoon light still too bright to see them clearly yet. She could see them best in the dark.

They moved through the worn path that cut though the layer of trees, bordering the long stretch of tidal flats at her ocean's doorstep. She knows the children never come here in the dark, though she aches for them.

She followed. Crouching in her heavy mass of hunger and shrouded by thick forest, she closed her eyes, exhaling deeply. She waited.

Children now getting close to dusk. Within her reach.

The girl.

She could hear its heart drumming. She could see its wild mind, too strong to capture because of what had just been done. She knew this child who held the rock would return someday. She would return to see through the eyes of the Wild Woman.

1.

Eggshells.

On a beautiful spring morning in May of 2001, I walked into the Fraser Valley feed store and there he was. Just a little rag of a rooster. I knew better, but I had to take him home anyway. He always fertilizes the eggs now. I thought of trying to hatch some of them, so I put them in a nesting box for one of my broody girls. She took to them just fine, but then the dog got into the coop. That poor hen died protecting her nest. So now here I am, standing in my kitchen, looking at the eggs I've gathered after the massacre. I don't really know how long I've been standing here for.

There's a small wisp of feather stuck to one of them, from the soft underside of their dead mother. There was something really sad about that one tiny feather. I remembered that finding one is supposed to mean something. Something spiritual. An angel is with you.

There are no angels here.

You can tell something is dead on the inside by looking at it. I was a good example of that. I picked up one of the eggs. Solid. Heavier than I thought it would be.

Dead weight soon.

I looked at the clock. Tally would be getting off the bus from school soon. I quickly gathered up the eggs, strolled outside, and threw them unceremoniously into the blackberry bushes behind the coop. No use in trying now. I'm not broody enough.

When you cut their heads off they run. It's a fact. I watched from the windy beach, on the north end of Vancouver Island, where we lived for most of my childhood years. My dad would have his shirt off. The stump solidly placed in the sand just as if the tree had died there. I watched because I didn't really believe what was happening, not the first time anyway. My long, dark hair whipping in front of my eyes, as if to try and blind me from the horror.

I was told it was my job to pull out the feathers. I didn't protest. I liked feathers. I would search for them on the beach all the time. A boy in my class told me I wasn't allowed to keep the ones I found if they're eagle feathers. I never asked him why. He seemed to be an authority on the matter.

The sound of the axe hitting the stump. The gruesome moment when you realize there's a body running with no head. No head, no brains. I stood on that beach as my dad whacked at their necks with his axe, wondering *how does the chicken know that it needs to run away if it doesn't have any brains anymore*?

I ran away once. I felt stupid and defeated for doing it. I didn't know where to go and I didn't get far anyway. Nobody wanted me.

I've been told that I passed out on the beach after the last chicken's head hit the sand. The men in that group of friends my parents had, they all laughed about it.

I would come to be known as the kid who has blackouts when stressed.

Run chicken run.

I look out the front window to see the dog running up the driveway to meet her. As they run toward the house together, Tally's auburn curls look wild.

She dropped her backpack, slamming the door behind her with as much force as she could to make her presence known. I don't waste my breath telling her to stop anymore. She'll just do it harder every time.

"Did you already get the eggs Mom?"

"Yeah I did honey. You hungry?"

"Starving! That sandwich smelled gross in my lunch, so I threw it out! I almost barfed."

I turn my head so she can't see me roll my eyes, and face the mess in the kitchen.

Why can't I ever get a handle on this?

The kitchen is a self-portrait of me these days. Disgusting. I manage to find a semi-clean pan, a few slices of bread and a chunk of hard cheese. At least someone here has an appetite. I'm thinking about the dying embryos in the blackberry bushes.

What will eat them?

"How was school today?"

She shrugs, looking out through the kitchen window.

Casting her fishing line.

Sure. I'll take the bait.

I let out a deep sigh, tossing a slice of bread with some cheese into the pan already on the stove and cast a tired glance in her direction.

"What's up? What happened?"

She turns toward me and stares, cool green eyes piercing mine. Dramatic effect well played.

"Daniel kicked me in the...you know...down there."

She sneers, staring intently, waiting for my reaction.

"Then kick him back."

She slowly leans back in her chair, crossing her arms and cocking her head to one side.

"Seriously? Won't I just get in trouble like always?"

I sigh. I can't tell her that walking away will stop it from happening. That would be a lie.

"I guess you only have two choices then. You let them kick you and do nothing about it and they'll just keep coming at you, or you kick back. The little jerk might learn his lesson. Don't let anyone think they can do that to you."

She sniffs and her eyes glow a little. I don't even ask her why it happened. I know that she's often an instigator. It's probably genetic with that hot Scottish blood. I think I can actually feel it coursing through my own sometimes. I pass off the grilled cheese sandwich to her at the same time my cell phone is vibrating on the table.

Three missed calls from him.

I take a breath and hold it for a moment.

Steady.

"Hey sorry about that, what's up?"

"For Christ's sake why are you always so hard to get a hold of! Aren't you at home?"

Of course I am. You know that. I have nowhere else to go.

We could just put this exchange on automatic recording. Always the same. I'm fighting the urge to tear into him. I just don't have the energy for this today. And Tally is listening. I breathe in as deeply as I can.

"What do you need?"

"A drink. I'm coming home early."

"Oh."

"What? That's it? Oh?" He grunts. "We need to talk when I get there."

I want to tell him that this demand really messes with my plans to escape the disaster in the house this afternoon and run screaming into the woods for a while.

To escape my life.

"I just wasn't expecting you home this early, Damien."

Whatever. I could use a drink too. I'll play along with him.

But my head wasn't clear enough for this. I wish I could just get out. I've been dragging myself around in this bullshit for too long.

"Talk to you in about an hour," he snaps, hanging up.

I put my phone down, aware of the headache starting to creep behind my neck.

We'll have nothing to really say to each other and we'll just sit with that spark of resentment we both hold. I thought I knew once why I keep trying. I can't think of a reason anymore.

I glance at the clock hopeful it would agree with me. We had at least an hour to get out of here before we start to lose daylight. Before he rolls in and it gets dark.

"Tally, finish up and we'll go for a quick hike before your dad gets home okay?"

She looks up at me, reading my level of enthusiasm.

If I'm too eager, she'll resist.

I turn to the sink and start washing some dishes. It helps not to make eye contact.

"Okay, let's go Mom."

I breathe out. Sometimes I don't even realize I'm holding my breath as long as I do.

The air has a cool, damp feeling to it already. I don't mind it though. I never liked using the trail behind our house in the heat, it drives the mosquitos mad for my blood. Tally whined and begged me to bring the dog with us, and she kept it up all the way to the lower steps, down past the trail opening. I lost count of how many times I'd said no. That dog doesn't listen and

I'm not chasing him around in the woods. Not to mention he'd flush out the eggs I aborted earlier.

I'm not risking any distractions out here. Not this late in the day.

I start walking a little faster. It could still be light enough by the time we reach the ravine, but only if we really hustle. Tally settles alongside my stride and starts her usual chatter, mixed with a dramatic shriek when we see a large slug across our path. I was never like that, all squeamish about bugs and slugs. I should have squashed that in her a long time ago.

I pondered for a moment in my own head, how much of who we are is shaped by our surroundings versus what we are born with. But does it even matter in the end? We all just end up trying to survive. To feel like we're allowed to take up space. And then we disappear anyway.

"MOM!"

Tally is shrieking and clawing at my arm.

I feel my consciousness surge back to the trail and look up toward the cracking sound above. A large branch was coming down fast, just a step ahead of us on our path.

"LOOK!"

She's pointing up into the trees, eyes wide.

I waited for the branch to crash, anxious for more cracking to come from above.

"Yeah, it's okay, it happens sometimes." I tried to sound calm.

Holy shit that was close!

"I'm just glad it didn't fall on us Tally!"

"No Mom, not that. Did you see him?"

My focus suddenly blurs.

See who?

"Who are you talking about?"

"That owl! I think it's the one from on the fence yesterday! He's following us!"

Was it starting to get dark already?

Sometimes it's hard to tell under thick forest. The air did feel much colder suddenly. My heart was still pounding from the fallen branch.

"Well, there you go, you got to see the owl again today. Hey, let's go back. I don't think I'm up for the whole hike anyways. I'm really tired."

She scowls. Hard.

"We have to go to the edge and throw our rocks. Mom! Please? We're almost there!"

She knows I will give in. I always give in.

We started doing this ritual hike a while back when I needed a way of redirecting her rage from daily social conflicts. From the struggle between her dad and I. From the frustrations of life as a girl.

To redirect my rage.

We usually make our way up to the ravine a few times a week to squeeze bad feelings into a rock in our hand. Then we throw it, sometimes releasing it with a scream. There's an echo.

She really needed to throw those rocks today. I decided we'd better go throw them then.

I know when to heed warnings.

Sometimes.

As we move down the trail, my mind wanders back to when I took a run up here on my own a while ago and picked up a rock about the size of an egg, dark gray with embedded opaque fragments. A rare moment for me to stand still and look with intent. There was something about all the compressed little fragments that made up that rock. I found it comforting. I stood on the edge of the trail at the bend in the switchback, overlooking the ravine for what seemed like a long time. I thought how odd it was that the rock had suddenly become so hot in the palm of my hand. I don't know why, or what I was thinking about, but the tears came and those were hot on my skin too. I don't even know what I was crying about. I just dropped that rock and walked home. I recall looking over my shoulder a few more times than usual on my way back that day.

I know I keep leaving something behind in the woods. Something I need to remember.

That's really why I keep going back I guess.

Now as Tally spits and growls at the edge of the ravine, I scan the trees for an audience. Nothing moves. I didn't even pay much attention to what she was carrying on about. I wait for her to start walking back toward home and I follow. She's quiet now. I tread softly, without words.

I heard his truck pull up like I always do. Heavy door slamming. Boots on the front landing. I quickly pour a generous glass of whiskey and pick up a bottle of red wine off the bar, pouring a half glass.

"Dad!"

Tally shrieked and jumped into his arms, squeezing him around the neck as hard as she could.

"I saw an owl today on the trail."

He put her down and dropped his jacket on the stairs.

"Wow, you did eh? When did you go on the trail?"

"We just got back. Oh, and Mom almost got killed by a tree."

He looked at me, one eyebrow raised. I raised an eyebrow back and shook my head. I grabbed the drinks and moved to the table, as she let go of him and bounced toward the door.

"I'm going to check on the chickens, Dad!"

I started to open my mouth to tell her to put her sweater on and then I stopped myself. It wasn't worth the energy.

"So what did you do today, besides dodging sudden death on the trail?"

He's using a mocking tone before he takes the first sip of his drink. I'm already feeling annoyed.

"The dog got into the coop again."

"How did he get in this time?"

"I don't know. The gate I guess. The latch doesn't stay down. You know I told you it needed to be fixed right?"

"It latches fine."

There it is. I'm already starting to hold my breath.

"Okay, well anyway after I fed them, I went back in the house to try and get some things done and next thing I know he's in there and he's got one. The poor thing wasn't dead yet when I got out there."

Stop talking. He doesn't care.

I sit up a little straighter once I realize I'm slouched over. I don't know why I always make myself small when I'm with him.

He gives me that look. That look that says *was that the hardest thing you had to deal with today? Another excuse for this mess of a place. Or is it just you being you?*

He takes a long sip. Then looks at me with his jaw set.

"I'm not going into work tomorrow. I'm going to go look at a truck. What are you doing?"

"Uh...I'm doing the usual. Getting Tally to school. I should try to get some writing done I guess. I haven't had time for anything."

He put the glass to his lips and swallowed the rest in one shot. He looked me up and down and I felt the shift. Faster than usual this time. The energy in the room like a snap of static.

"What the hell do you do that makes you so tired? Don't you have all day to get shit done around here while she's in school? What the hell! Seriously Cora?!"

"I didn't say I was tired."

I could hear my voice crack.

Dammit.

I ball my fists up under the table and squeeze hard.

He's glaring at me. I look away. Aware that I'm setting my jaw now, grinding my teeth a little. He stands up and sets his glass down hard.

"I'm going out. Enough of this shit with you. It's not worth it."

He left me to watch the last bit of daylight being taken by dusk on my own.

Tally wandered out of the chicken coop. With a slight pause, she watched her dad get into his truck. Then she carried on into the house, her voice trailing with a song.

At least I wouldn't have to fight with her to come in and get ready for dinner and bed.

I don't want to fight with anyone, anymore.

Lying on my back, half listening to her tell the usual bedtime story, this time it ends with Odin the Owl landing on my head and biting my nose off my face. I wonder if I should be worried about her sense of gratification. I feel myself drifting off to sleep.

"Mom?"

Slowly, I roll onto my side and face her. Half awake.

"When I went in the coop some of the eggs were cracked open."

"Hm. Or did you just drop them again?"

"No I swear. There were three already broken."

Three more? Wow they were on a roll today!

"Well sometimes chickens will peck at them. Maybe they're stressed out."

Tally laughs out loud, curling her knees up to her chest, rolling with laughter at my suggestion.

"Mom! Chickens don't get stressed out!"

"Why not? Especially the mammas do. If you had to take care of babies growing in those fragile little eggs, you'd probably get stressed out too."

"No, I'd just eat them."

I roll over onto my back, closing my eyes. I'm too tired to take the bait on that weird conversation.

"Okay Tally go to sleep."

I really have to get some laundry done.

I wait until I can hear her breathing deeply before I force myself to get up.

I pick up my glass of wine and head down to the laundry room. I stand in the doorway and stare at the piles on the floor, clumps of laundry left on top of the machines, more probably inside the washer, building up a good stench from being left there for too long.

I've been left here for too long.

I took a long sip from my glass. The wine is acidic and burns going down. In silent protest, I turn my back on the mess.

I figured if I read for a while until sleep takes over, then I might wake up with some spark of motivation and get some writing done. Push a button on a machine. Something. Anything.

All of this will still be here for me tomorrow anyway. Nothing ever changes.

2.

Boots.

I am surrounded in tall, thick trees. It's dark, and there's light from the moon coming through the ceiling of branches, enough that I can see where I need to run... oh my God I need to run...

RUN!

I'm trying to look ahead at the same time I'm watching for what's coming for me from behind. The anxiety in my chest like heavy stones. My legs are lead, my breathing hard and fast. Thick, damp, salty air blankets my skin. As I whip my head around to see, I lose my footing, falling in slow motion. Crashing down heavily into a bed of dark soil and thick moss, dirt flies into my mouth, then sprays out with spit as I release the scream that's building up in my head. I'm clawing at the dirt, desperate to grab onto something inside the earth and hold myself down from being ripped away. The thing I'm running from is close now. I can feel it.

I can't get up and run anymore. I'm too heavy with fear. I can only scream,

and scream,

and scream...

and then I feel small hands slapping on my back and a high pitched voice squalling in my ear, "Mom! Stop it!"

I open my eyes, heart pounding with a wave of adrenaline leaving my body. Light from the bedside lamp is blinding. Tally is standing over me with wide eyes, her lips hard pressed together.

"Tally hey, what? What is it?"

She lets out a huff. "I can't sleep when you're so loud!!"

I pull myself up and push the covers off. There's a cold chill in the room.

I forgot to turn on the heat.

My mouth is dry. I rub my temples hard.

"I'm sorry, go back to bed please. Everything is fine."

"Where's Dad?"

I look to the other side of the bed, not surprised to see that it's empty.

"He'll be home soon. Go back to bed."

She walks out of the room, leaving me half coherent and yet awake, with a familiar sense that I've left my nightmare once again without an ending. I reach for my glass on the nightstand, take a sip of the stale water that's been left there, lay back down, and stare up at the ceiling. Still so tired, I easily close my eyes and hope for nothing to come.

The morning light floats through the window and creeps up on my shoulder.

I'm aware that it's unusually quiet.

Why is that rooster so quiet?

There hasn't been a morning yet where he's neglected us with his annoying call.

I'm about to make my way out to the coop with their feed and quickly decide Tally can take care of it instead. Grateful to just greet the coffee maker and sit in a comatose state for the better part of the morning, I shuffle into the kitchen. Seeing his large dirty boots kicked off in the middle of the kitchen floor immediately grates on my nerves.

He knows I hate that.

"Damien?"

No answer.

He probably came home early this morning and just crashed on the couch.

My brain calls for coffee before concern over whatever it is he was up to last night or what pathetic state he'll be in this morning. Noting that at least he didn't come home in one of his drunken fighting moods, I satisfy myself with kicking his boots aside on the kitchen floor. Tally's bedroom door opens and my attention quickly shifts back to my need for that coffee. I start filling the pot with tap water while she rummages in the pantry for cereal.

"Good morning honey. Sorry I woke you up last night."

She continues to set herself up for breakfast, ignoring me and pulling a spoon out of the drawer. She pulls out the milk and closes the fridge door with a little more force than necessary.

I turn away, careful again. Eggshells.

"Hey Tally, did you already go out and feed the chickens this morning?"

She sits down at the table, balancing an overflowing bowl with milk skirting the rim.

"Nope."

"Okay I thought maybe you did. I didn't hear the rooster this morning, did you?"

She doesn't respond, and continues to shovel cereal dripping with milk into her mouth.

Letting out a deep sigh, I continue my efforts for coffee. I load a few extra grinds in the filter, inhaling the aroma. I'm well rehearsed at knowing when this girl is in one of her moods. It's not a good time to have any shred of conversation. I exhale, relieved to see she's already dressed for school.

So that's one battle that will not be in the queue for today.

After a few quick gulps of coffee, I slip on my boots and walk out toward the coop with some pellets for the chickens. I can see the hens start to squabble and stir themselves up the closer I get. Then I see him. The mass of black feathers on the rooster's body, laying like a limp, mud smeared rag on the ground. The hens clamber all over him. He doesn't move under the chaos. I set my bucket down, and grab a few handfuls of feed to disburse the girls.

"Couldn't handle the ladies anymore or what, hey buddy?"

I stand over him, waiting for any sign of life. If he had even one second of fight left in him, I wanted to know before I tried to pick him up. I kicked him over gently with my boot. His head lolled to one side, eyes open, blank and staring at me. Blood trickling from his sharp, opaque beak. I counted the hens. The last time something got into the coop, aside from the dog, it had ripped the head off of one. However, the girls had all kept their heads this morning. With no time to dispose of his corpse before pushing Tally off to catch the bus, I mentally make note of my grim chore to put on the never-ending to-do-list for the day. I picked up the shovel that was leaning on the fence and scooped up his body. Surprised by the heaviness of his dead weight, I parked the carcass in the corner of the coop and positioned the shovel head to cover him up from the hens as best I could for now. I would come out and bury him later.

I stepped back into the house to remind Tally that her bus is coming in a few minutes. She stuffed her lunch bag in her back-pack and pulled her boots on.

"We didn't hear the rooster this morning Tally, because something happened to him last night."

She looked up at me with a steady gaze.

"I know. I killed him yesterday."

I met her gaze.

"What do you mean YOU killed him?"

"He's always attacking me! And he's always hurting the other chickens! It was kind of an accident."

"Oh my God! How? What did you do? Why didn't you tell me?"

She rolls her eyes.

"Whatever. It's not a big deal. He was trying to get me again so I used the shovel to stop him and I hit him really hard with it. He didn't like... die right away. So I hit him again."

She flashed her narrowed eyes at me. Challenging me on her decision.

"Tal... I can't even process this right now. I can't believe you didn't tell me about this! You had to kill him? Why didn't you just call us to help you if he was attacking you?"

She put her hands on her hips and scowled.

"You guys were having one of your stupid fights! Anyway, who cares."

I stand in front of her, blocking the front door, stunned at this casual declaration that she's killed our rooster.

What do I do with this?

She was right, he was vicious. I had to ward him off with a shovel a few times myself.

But killing him was avoidable.

I was stunned with the shock of hearing her confession. Assured of my submission over the matter, she picked up her backpack and moved toward the door.

"So when I get home I'll just do a funeral for him, okay Mom?"

She's suddenly cheerful with the prospect of this plan. It's settled.

I take a step back from the door as she gathers her things to head for the bus. A bit of relief washes over me that she seems to have enough decency (*or remorse?*) to be planning a burial event for the poor thing.

Had she planned to kill it or was it just an accident?

"Okay. I think that's a good idea."

There wasn't anything else I could say in that moment. I watch her skip down the driveway to meet the bus.

I finally decide to put some laundry through a cycle and go for a run on the trail. I haven't taken advantage of some solitude for a while. Then maybe I'll return to find a spark of motivation to produce some work to submit. I haven't been able to write for a few months now.

I take a glance in the living room before I go, and see that Damien is in fact sprawled out on the couch, still wearing his jacket, jeans, and his dirty ball cap.

I'd like to hit him with that shovel a few times.

Just the thought is enough for now.

I escape the house as quickly and as quietly as I can, avoiding confrontation.

The trail entrance behind our house smells sweet and earthy, a densely wooded area that I love. It's the reason we bought this house when Tally was a baby. Damien's mother was adamant we should immediately fence the backyard, or we would risk having Tally wander off into the woods or worse, have a wild animal drag her off. This declaration was paired with her sweeping criticisms and bleating about "the constant mess our baby has to live in and how can you possibly keep an eye on things and sit in that office doing whatever you do?" I was never sure if she was talking about my baby or hers. That woman had her not-so-subtle ways of insulting my capabilities as a mother and a wife in one fell swoop. After all, nothing was ever good enough for dear Damien. She had passed away last summer. I still didn't feel free. Her words always cut so deep they left scars.

Run faster.

It didn't take long for my adrenaline to kick in once those thoughts started rolling around in my head.

There are moments when the timing of your footing has to be just right over the roots that creep across the path or you might trip and chance cracking a bone. My overactive imagination gets the best of me out here, where I think in that moment a cougar might leap out and sink its teeth into my jugular. I would surely die, suffocating in my own blood as it floods my throat.

I would be free.

Even though the thought of this doesn't seem so terrible on a day like today, it does make me run a little faster, which of course then makes it harder to navigate the uneven trail and my risk of falling. But I felt like I needed to really push it today. Just fly.

I reach the midpoint of the trail where the bend in the switchback sits on the edge of the ravine. This is the furthest I ever take Tally on our hikes. I find a tree to lean on and catch my breath, letting the blood slow down that's rushing to my brain. My hands were numb. Shaking them to get some feeling back, I look out over the ravine.

Breathing steady now, I remind myself that I don't want to stop for too long or I'll lose that high that I love once it kicks in. But there's something in the air today that has me noticing the quiet. The soft rustle of the breeze in the trees as it seduces the leaves. The space in this moment is so calming, comforting. My breathing slows with a sudden feeling of overwhelming sadness for that rooster. Animals don't deserve to suffer.

But some people do.

I'm feeling lightheaded. Very lightheaded.

I lower myself to the ground, putting my head between my knees.

Everything goes black.

I'm six years old. I'm riding in the truck with my dad to our camp. It's a rough ride down a long gravel road toward the mouth of the river on the north end of Vancouver Island. It's summertime and the mosquitos are thirsty. I'm scratching incessantly, my skin covered in welts and scabs. We're keeping our chickens at the camp. One has been born with a deformed leg. I'm a faithful visitor at the coop because of this one. They're all crammed in a large wire cage with no shelter. Dad says meat chickens don't get the luxury of building materials to shelter them. Their lives are too short to bother with all of that. I watch this little chick trying constantly to escape the hard, incessant stabbing from the others. The top of its head is pink with pecked over meat. Looking at me, pleading with me to save it, I'm sure of this. I beg my dad for a rescue mission. He reluctantly stops his work and rolls out a small wire mesh enclosure off to the side of the larger cage, and deposits the sad little thing into this refuge. I feed the tiny bird generous scoops of scraps and pellets. There's an enormous sense of satisfaction and justice having been served here, and it sets down roots deep within my core. That night, I fall very ill. Fevered for days, blotted in Calamine lotion and in a sleepy, constant dose of Tylenol, I had to abandon my rescue mission. When my crusted over blisters soon signal recovery, my mom insists I try my appetite for dinner at the kitchen table. I sit down. We're having roast chicken. There are three bodies on the table. One is smaller than the others. I'm sure I know why. I vomit all over my plate.

Wake up.

I'm on my side in the scattered rocks and dirt just off the edge of the trail, aware of a cold sweat covering my face and back.

Did I hit my head?

I can taste vomit in my mouth, then see it spilled out over the ground in front of my face. Thankful for gravity and the good fortune of having rolled onto my side somehow. With a sense of momentary panic, I wonder how long I've been out for. Sitting up, head throbbing, I look at my watch. Noon. A sigh of relief as there's plenty of time to head back and get cleaned up before Tally gets home.

I make a mental note that I should probably call my doctor for another appointment.

Maybe I do need to start that medication. I haven't ever been sick from an episode like this.

I quickly dismiss the thought, deciding it's likely just the result of an overly strenuous run. Feeling exhausted, I slowly start back down the trail. Wondering if Damien would still be at the house now. I'm annoyed with myself for not being able to remember his work schedule. Then I recall his comment about not working today and telling me that he's buying another truck.

Not asking me.

Going over the list of things in my head that I need to pay attention to for the remainder of the day, he's not one of them. The first thing I'm hoping to see when I get home are his boots off the kitchen floor. And gone.

3.

Blackout.

Walking up the porch steps, I stomp the dirt off my runners and open the back door to the kitchen. I can already see Damien's boots still lying in the middle of the floor. It's quiet. He's either still passed out on the couch or he's gone and didn't bother picking up after himself, as usual.

I stand still. Waiting to hear him.

I'm not picking up those goddam boots for him again.

My phone vibrates on the kitchen counter.

"Hello?"

"Cora! I've called you three times! Where the hell have you been? You're not answering your cell again for Christ's sake."

I hold the phone away from my ear to keep Damien's words from hammering into my skull.

Right. He's not wearing work boots today.

"I was out for a run."

"Well, I'm at the shop with my truck. The school just called. I can't leave and the principal wants you to go in and see him."

"Why? What happened?"

"He wouldn't say why. Just get in there and see what's going on. Call me back after you do that."

"Okay. When will you be home?"

He's already hanging up.

Why is it always me that has to deal?

After a once-over with a facecloth at the bathroom sink, I quickly grab my keys and head to the car.

Sitting outside the office waiting for the principal to finish a phone call, I can only imagine what the issue is. Tally is nowhere in sight. I didn't bother to go to her classroom first, unsure of what to do. The drama with her can wait anyway. I straighten out my spine as I sit in the chair, aware of my shallow breath. Elementary school still had that same cold feeling mine did, with the classroom artwork stapled up along the walls outside the office to overcome the grey waxed floors and dull beige walls. I used to love being the one who got to smash my palm against the stapler into the wall, while my classmate positioned the artwork. Later there was always an overwhelming urge to rip it down whenever I'd walk past.

Smirking a little, still tempted now. I look up toward the large white-faced clock on the wall, ticking.

Chatty today aren't we, Mr. Principal?

Tick... tick... tick...

More memories started to creep into my mind. Feeling heavy, I decided to close my eyes. Just for a minute.

I'm eleven years old and rigid with anticipation, watching the Elder shuffle into our classroom just before we were released for the afternoon into the fresh north island air. She speaks with a low, hoarse voice and holds a cedar mask adorned with long, wiry, black hair, deep set pinhole eyes on a red and black face. Our eager minds were entranced with her story as she slowly leans toward us.

"Wild Woman of the Woods. She wanders amongst the ancient trees with her large cedar basket, searching for children to carry off. If you're bad, she will get you. If you wander after dark into the woods, she will find you and eat you. Pay careful attention, don't go too far into the woods. Listen for the owls to give a warning call. Even then it might be too late! Keep out when the darkness comes."

After school, I wanted to take the longer route home. Even though it went deeper into the forest, we had plenty of daylight left and the salmonberries were sweeter there. My best friend, Shaina, agreed. Walking the dense trail home, I tell her I was sure that something was watching us. Following us. I knew the story that the Elder had spoken of just had to be true. Our nervous chatter held within the wall of trees around us. When we heard something moving through the forest, our imaginations went wild. Shaina peed herself.

Three older boys from our trailer park stopped us on our path. They noticed her wet pants, laughing and moving slowly toward us. Circling, like hyenas.

I wailed at them, "Go away! Leave us alone!"

"Come here baby." They continue to laugh as they circle us.

I remember getting home and it was starting to get dark. I don't remember much of anything in between.

Why?

Maybe the first of one of my blackouts.

I try to remember everything from that day sometimes. It wasn't an unusual day. We had followed the trail from school to home often, though sometimes we strayed and took the longer route. But there was something missing. I've always brushed it off as memory loss as the years go on. I've never talked about it with Shaina. I don't know why. Maybe just another day of navigating the usual childhood dirt.

Except now as I sit here at Tally's school, drifting from consciousness, I remember something about those boys.

I feel a heavy hand on my shoulder. I snap my eyes open and look up. The principal was standing over me.

"Mrs. Brochan, are you alright?"

Clearing my throat, I stood up, rubbing my temples.

"Yes, sorry I didn't hear you come out. You called my husband?"

"Yes I did after I couldn't reach you. I'd like to speak with you about an incident. Come in, please."

I followed him into his office, making eye contact with the secretary as she walked out of the back storage room, her arms heavy with stacks of printer sheets, giving me a sympathetic half smile. I sat myself down across from his desk, sitting up as straight as possible. My chair seemed to be at a much lower height than his was.

"Mrs. Brochan, we had a serious incident with your daughter at lunch hour concerning another student. She admittedly assaulted him by kicking him in the private parts."

I sucked in my breath.

Careful Cora. It's not time to celebrate your daughter's victory quite yet.

I cleared my throat and tried to relax my jaw.

"What happened exactly? Did she just randomly kick this boy or was he provoking her in some way?"

The principal shifted uncomfortably in his chair and avoided my gaze.

Of course she was provoked. That's usually the case in this situation. It's self defense. Okay, let's hear it big man.

"Unfortunately Mrs. Brochan, there were no witnesses and it's your daughter's word against the other student's, who's injuries I might add are palpable. He claims he did nothing toward her to warrant this assault. Regardless, her actions would never be excusable."

He waves his hand in the air in a dismissive way as he continues to deliver his speech.

"Your daughter doesn't appear to be injured. She's quite adamant that what she did was a justifiable action, claiming you had in fact directed her to do so."

Oh. Right.

"I guess I should have reported to you earlier that Tally did tell me she's been having some difficulty with a boy from her class. If this is the same boy involved that she's complained to me about, then yes I did tell her it was perfectly acceptable to use self defense if she's being physically assaulted in any way. I'm sure you'd agree that would be reasonable action to take."

The clock on the wall seemed loud in the awkward silence as he took a moment to respond.

"Mrs. Brochan, I don't recommend that our students use physical harm to solve their personal problems. I would appreciate it if you would encourage your daughter to speak with an adult on the school grounds if she encounters any further difficulty."

He folds his hands on his desk and continues.

"I'm sure he was just teasing her because he likes her. Surely, you can remember how that goes at this age." He nods, satisfied with his position on the matter.

Heat rises from my stomach, my jaw clenches, face starts to burn.

I should leave now. Exit stage left.

"Well I have no doubt that he won't be bothering my daughter anymore. Are we finished here?"

He looks at me for a moment and then opens his mouth to say something, but closes it. He takes out a yellow slip of paper. As he's writing, the bell goes off.

I decide I might as well pull her out from the bus line while I'm here, we'll go run some errands, maybe get some ice cream.

I wait to be dismissed.

"I'm giving Tallulah a yellow slip. A warning for misconduct. This incident will be on her student record. I expect that you and your husband will have some conversation with her immediately, regarding appropriate behaviour toward other students."

I've got some misconduct I'd like to show you. Smug asshole!

He hands me the slip. I take it.

"Of course." I smile sweetly.

I didn't bother to talk to Tally about the incident. We finish errands and head home, pulling into the driveway with Damien right behind us, in his new truck. Music thumping.

Tally jumps out and runs over to him. I can tell he's in a good mood if the music is loud. He gets out and puts her in a head lock. She laughs. He reaches into the truck and pulls a case of beer out of the back. I walk into the house, pull the yellow slip out of my pocket and throw it in the garbage. As they both walk in together, she's chattering to him about what happened at school. He looks at me, not really listening to her.

"You didn't call me back."

I shrug my shoulders and shake my head slightly.

Please don't. Not now.

"Damien, I just finished with the principal and then we got busy. It really wasn't a big deal. Just a little problem with another kid."

He looks down at Tally, who's still stuck to him like a magnet. He places his hand on the top of her head.

"What kind of problem?"

"Josh from my class was trying to push me down off the playground again and telling me to eat dirt! So I kicked him down there. As hard as I could."

Damien runs his hand through his hair and sighs.

"Mom told me to do it, so he'd stop bugging me."

A half grin creeps across her face. She makes eye contact with me, as if we might share a secret code with each other. I can feel Damien's glare.

"What kind of thing is that to tell her to do, Cora?!"

I don't look at him. Instead, I look at Tally and enjoy this rare moment we've connected. He interrupts.

"Next time just tell the kid to back off or your dad will take care of him. Your mom shouldn't have told you to do that. That was stupid. Got it?"

She shrugs her shoulders. "Okay."

I can feel the heat creeping into my face.

To hell with you and your egotistical bullshit Damien. Kick them where it hurts. That's the only way to make the little bastards stop.

He looks at me and gives a dismissive grunt, takes off his shoes, and carries his beer into the living room with Tally skipping after him. A cup of strong, steeped tea and some solitude in the office would be good for me, while he's got her attention.

I need to write. I need to try.

It was almost too hot to wrap my hands around the cup, but the sting of heat felt good. Sitting at my desk, looking out the window, I watched the tree line at the back of the property. It was strange how that memory came up for me at the school today. When we used to walk in those woods back then, the only rule was to be home before dark. That was it. Even with bears, cougars, and who knows what else?

I blow gingerly on the steaming cup of tea, scan the darkening sky, and notice the moon emerging before I settle into my notebook. The wind was picking up outside, the trees were starting to sway. My eyes traced the tree line, catching the large owl perched on the last fencepost. Its head turned, and it sent a hard stare back at me through the window. Suddenly, my eyes blur and my mind feels heavy. I'm overwhelmed with the urge to call my friend, Shaina.

But I decided to wait until I was sure Tally was asleep.

It's been a while since we've talked. I don't want to be interrupted. We have a lot to catch up on.

Why haven't I called in so long? Why hasn't she?

4.

Flight.

Who can tell me what I can't remember?
Large yellow eyes said,
"The one who saw you."

I woke up painfully aware that my arm is asleep under the weight of my head, and notice my notebook open. There's writing on the page. I sit up and drop the pen still in my hand. My tea is cold. I don't hear Damien or Tally. I walk into the living room where both are asleep together on the couch. I quietly walk into the kitchen. The time on the stove is 3:45 a.m. The dog is scratching at the kitchen door. I open the door to let him out and then step outside. Breathing in the cool night air, I pull my phone from my pocket and scroll the contacts.

Shaina.

Ringing, three times.

I'm feeling anxious that she won't pick up. Why would she pick up in the middle of the night?

"Cora?"

"Oh God I'm waking you up I know I'm so sorry. I really needed to call you. I just really need to talk. I'm so sorry I haven't called in so long... I'm sorry... I..."

I feel my body starting to shake. It must be the cold air. I hear her sigh.

"Cora. It's okay. It's so good to hear your voice! I'm not really sleeping anyway. I'm just a night owl these days, on a few calls. It's been busy."

She laughs in her soft way. "How are you? You've been on my mind lately too."

I hear the hint of concern in her voice. She thinks she knows why I'm calling at this hour, like before. But not this time.

"Yeah everything is ok, nothing really going on. I'm just...."

But I can't explain.

Why am I calling her this late?

"Cora. You can tell me. If you and Tally need to come and stay again I'm here for you, don't worry about that."

"No, no it's not that. I just keep feeling like I need to get out of here. Just for a break. I don't know what's happening. I'm just not myself lately and..."

I'm choking back emotions for reasons I don't have.

Breathe. Tell her. About remembering.

"Shaina, listen I think I'm going to grab some of my things here and just drive. I'll head your way and stay for a couple of days. Then we can talk. Is that okay?"

"Of course. I'll be here. Keep me posted okay? Are you bringing Tally and are you telling Damien?"

"Yeah I'll text him once I'm gone. I think he can take on Tally for a couple days. It'll be good for him and for me."

Shaina agrees, and we hang up. The house is still quiet. The dog follows me inside and lays down on his blanket in the kitchen.

Good boy.

Careful not to make a sound, I pack a few clothes, grab my coat, my keys, and go before I can't.

I'll text him in the morning. It's not like he always lets me know when he's coming or going, so how is it any different if I just take off?

But it is different. I know it is.

My car won't start. I try turning the key again.

Click click click.

Seriously?!

I get out and open the hood.

A feeling of hopelessness mixed with panic starts to settle in. I'm feeling lightheaded. I squat down and put my head between my knees.

It didn't look like I was going to run off anywhere after all.

I've always loved to run. For as long as I can remember, I would just run. Down long stretches of road, through the trails. Anywhere, anytime. It was like breaking through some brick wall inside of me once I hit that high of adrenaline and left everyone behind. In school, always leading the pack. Effortless. I was a few years older than Tally when our family had to leave the north end of the island and move to the city. I remember the feeling of satisfaction when I arrived to outrun everyone in my new class. I remember the hate too. The boys called me thunder thighs. How they noticed my breasts. How they grabbed at me. How I tried to stop them. I kicked one so hard he threw up. Then his friends all ran and told on me. I remember how the principal looked me up and down as I tried to explain it was worth it to defend myself, but the look on his face told me what I was worth. When I got home I was locked in my room, grounded for embarrassing behavior. I remember my whole body on the door. Two hands trying hard to open the locked doorknob. I just wanted to run. Then I remember waking up on the floor of my bedroom.

My battery is dead?

I stood up in front of my car slowly. If this was a dead battery, I couldn't exactly pull out the jumper cables and fire up his truck in the middle of the night. He'd likely wake up and then I wouldn't be going anywhere.

Damien had taken my car a few weeks ago and was late coming home because he said my battery had a loose connection so he couldn't start it. He said, "Just jiggle the battery wire if it dies again, it'll be fine."

I have a loose battery connection.

I look under the hood and jiggle the wires connected to the battery.

I turn the key. Nothing.

I sink into the driver's seat and fix my eyes on the house. It's still dark. He's not coming for me. Yet.

I feel like I'm suddenly drowning. My breathing becomes shallow. Options flood my brain. I could just call a cab. I could take his truck.

Hell no! He would kill me!

I get out and try again, giving the battery cables a good hard twist on the terminals.

I turn the key.

It's running now.

I quickly close the hood and jump back into the driver's seat.

I inhale and back out of the driveway slowly, holding my breath. Before I take my exit, I look at the house one last time. Still dark.

Exhale.

The rush of adrenaline is electrifying. I'm awake. Headlights on. Window down. No music. I don't want noise. My head is humming. An hour passes quickly.

I make a mental note to text Damien in another hour or so once I hit the ferry terminal. Before he wakes up. Before he realizes what I've done and before he loses his mind over it.

I'll message him because I don't want Tally to worry about me.

What do I say? I just needed a break? I'm sorry? I'll be back soon?

I'd have to be back at least by Monday morning before she goes to school. I could just drive back Sunday night. Take the last ferry over from the island.

Or not.

I feel some kind of wild, hysterical laughter welling up inside of me and my vision starts to blur.

I quickly pull over to the side of the highway. Leaving the car running, I step out of the car door and slap my hands on the roof, throwing shrieks of laughter out over the bank off the highway. Clear vision again.

This is good. I can do this. I need to do this.

Closing my eyes, cupping my hands on my face, and pausing for a moment to maintain my focus, I look up. It's brighter now. The clouds have drifted away from the moon.

Almost a full moon. It's beautiful.

I pull the car away after shoulder checking three times, even though there hasn't been another soul on the road. My fuel gauge gives me the green light to make it to the ferry terminal. I settle in for the trip with Portishead's *Dummy* in the CD player.

I loved the fact that they beat Oasis for best album. Those whiny, pathetic men didn't deserve to be awarded for their inflated egos and shit music.

I hit the play button. The first song was the perfect song.

Numb. Thank-you Beth Gibbons.

The whole album plays through on my way to the terminal.

Pulling up to the ticket window for the 6:15 a.m. sailing, I hear my phone vibrate in my bag. I ignore it momentarily, stay focused on getting my boarding ticket, and then park the car in my lane. I know who it is before I even have to look.

The text abrasive on the screen, “Where are you?”

I should have texted him first. Doesn’t matter. He’s going to be livid no matter how or when he gets the message.

I call his number. He picks up after one ring.

“WHERE ARE YOU!!!”

I can hear the rage in his voice.

“I’m sorry I didn’t tell you first Damien. I just didn’t want to wake you up. I’m only gone for a few days. I’m going to see Shaina and I’ll be back for Monday morning so you don’t have to worry about getting Tally to school.”

“You can’t just leave! What the hell is going on this time! You don’t say anything?!”

I’m holding my phone away from my ear. I can hear him seething and spitting through his teeth.

“So what, did you plan this little escape with that basket-case friend of yours?! Now you’re both laughing at me right? You just up and leave me with this kid? I’ve got shit to deal with! This is not happening Cora!”

Yes. Yes, it is happening.

“Stop yelling you’ll wake up Tally.”

“I don’t give a shit! What kind of a mother does this? What

the hell is wrong with you? Come back here. NOW."

"No. I told you what I'm doing."

I can hear him breathing hard.

"Bitch."

He's gone. I stop myself from texting any further explanations or apologies.

They'll be fine. Tally is old enough and he can step up and be there for her. For once.

Suddenly I felt a chill. I thought about the possibility that he could come here before I would board. I checked the time. He wouldn't make it. I turn off my phone and lean back. Boarding soon.

5.

Wreckage.

Staring out the window at the white caps as the ferry cradles me across the water, my hands still on the steering wheel, I'm suddenly overwhelmed.

Guilt. *I just left without any warning!*

Disbelief. *Did I really just leave like that?*

Fear. *He's going to be really mad.*

Sadness. *Why does it have to be like this?*

I knew why.

Because that's just how it is. It was my fault for letting it continue on that way for so long. I felt drained. It's been too many years.

I left him once before and I took Tally with me. It was okay at first. We stayed with Shaina. But we couldn't do that forever. I couldn't support us with my writing. My parents were gone. He said he would stop. He promised it would get better. What was I supposed to do? It all feels like I've been on a fast moving train for too long. At first the trip looked exciting. I was lonely and rebounding from a previous relationship so I was quick to get on board. The promised destination looked so beautiful. False advertising. We never get there. So I'm always waiting and hoping that I can get off that train. But it just doesn't stop.

I met Damien at a car accident. It had to be the strangest place to meet your future spouse. I was heading home from my journalism class that evening when the truck ahead of me suddenly hit the brakes, skidding to a stop and smashing into the back of a minivan. Thankfully, I was paying attention before doing the same. An older woman, looking distressed, approached the driver's side window of the truck ahead of me. She was completely losing her mind, shrieking up into the window. The truck door opened, and he stepped out, took off his ball cap and shook his head. As the woman continued to scream and flail her arms. I stepped out of my car and shouted, "Hey do you need me to call 911?"

He turned to look at me, ignoring the shrieking woman, and came toward me.

"No, no not necessary. She's fine, just a bump."

He was about my age, clean shaven and so attractive.

Instant electricity.

Or was it just my adrenaline from witnessing the accident? I couldn't even hear the woman anymore. All I could see were light green eyes piercing through me. He smiled. Dimples. He turned back toward the woman. His voice calm and cool.

"Okay come on now. You're okay. Calm down. Let's put the crazy down, it's just a little fender bender."

He walked over to her minivan and she followed, still voicing her obvious distress. After a few moments, he returned to his truck and pulled paperwork from the glove box.

I was leaning on my car door, watching him.

“Are you sure everything is okay? You don’t need me to call an ambulance for her?”

He turned around and smiled again.

“Nah, she’ll be alright, no damage done. She just wants my info anyway. But just hold tight for a sec in case I want your info.”

He winked at me and walked back over to the minivan. I wasn’t sure he was being serious.

I sat in my car and waited, checking the rearview mirror. There was no oncoming traffic but I put my hazards on anyway. I checked the mirror again and decided I looked horrible. Rolling down the window for some air, I wondered why I didn’t put any make-up on today, and then I remembered that I don’t really wear make-up.

He came back toward my car and leaned in.

“Well, I guess I should probably take your number in case I need a witness or something.”

I smiled.

“Everything’s okay though?”

“Yeah, she said I was tailgating her so she hit the brakes and well, I guess that’s what you get then right! Crazy bitch.”

He shook his head and I nodded slightly.

He stood up and looked toward his truck, smacking his insurance papers in his hand.

"Okay." I sat up a little taller and tried to speak up before I lost my nerve. "I'll give you my number. You might need it after all."

He turned his head back toward me and flashed a grin.

A few months later I was pregnant.

He proposed immediately when I told him my pregnancy test results. His mother asked, "Why the rush?" Even though she got the news first because she happened to arrive at his place unannounced in that moment. My parents were excited when they heard next. We had a small backyard ceremony at their house.

When I was four months along, Damien and I had our first fight.

For the first few months of my pregnancy, it was all I could do to get myself out of bed every day. I was so sick. I tried saltine crackers, ginger-ale, crushed ice. Barely keeping any of it down. Damien left in the morning for work every day. When he came home one night he seemed agitated. I was laying on the couch and a bucket was my constant companion. He just looked at me lying there. He looked at me with disdain.

I could feel it.

"You know if you just get up and do something you'll feel better."

"Damien I can't. I have really bad morning sickness you know that. I just need to lie here. It'll go away soon maybe in another week or so. I'm sorry."

"Well what am I supposed to do? Sit around here and listen to you complain?"

He was raising his voice.

"I'm not complaining. I'm puking."

"This is fucking pathetic! You can get over it. It's all in your head. You're just being fucking lazy. So I'm just supposed to work for both of us and you're here lying around all day?"

I'm suddenly aware of how heavy my body is on the couch, sinking.

"Get your shit together Cora. I'm going out."

"Why? Where are you going? You just got home!"

Door slams. Truck starts.

I don't think I will ever be able to forget the feeling I had when I flipped my phone open an hour later and saw those words.

Those words he sent in a text.

"I don't want to do this. I'm not ready to be a father."

Or perhaps I did forget (forgive?) somehow, because I stayed. Even though he didn't come home that time for two days.

Tallulah Rowena Brochan couldn't wait until her due date to come screaming into the world. She was three weeks early and born on Monday, April 9th 1990. I called my mom first. I was so thankful to have my mom. Damien was at work and didn't make it in time. Apparently, I'm one of those women who wins the lottery with short labour because Tally arrived just under an hour after my first few contractions started. It helped that she was a tiny little thing at just five pounds two ounces. Tiny but shockingly strong, lifting her head when they put her on my chest.

Damien finally showed up, afraid to hold her. My mom brought her to him and cradled her into his arms.

"She's fine. She's strong like her mom. Listen to those lungs! Go on, you got her. Here's your little girl, Daddy."

It gets harder to remember my mom's sweet voice as the years go on. Tally doesn't remember her grandparents. She was three months old when my mom was on her way to our place to help me get some rest. I was exhausted. Damien wasn't coming home until late in the evenings and I wasn't getting any sleep. Tally was colicky.

A semi-truck ran a red light and hit my mom's car. They said she was killed instantly. I don't know why they even tell you that. Dad had a heart attack a week later, which actually brought me some peace in the midst of such shattering grief. They would still be together.

The ferry announcement is muffled through the sweatshirt I had wrapped around my head to block out the light. My neck had an agonizing cramp from the awkward position I fell asleep in.

PASSENGERS WE ARE ARRIVING AT THE TERMINAL. PLEASE RETURN TO YOUR VEHICLES.

My legs are tingling from a lack of circulation and my mouth is dry. I try to stretch and then reach for my phone to check for messages.

Nothing.

I don't know if I should feel relieved or worried.

Right now I feel like I should have taken a walk around before docking. No time now.

I close my eyes again and wait. Relieved to be back on the island again. Home.

Engines ahead start up. I reach for my keys, pulling my seat forward. Hoping for less drama than earlier, I turn the key.

I give a little cheer when it fires up on the first try.

Driving the Island Highway is like seeing an old friend. We're together again, singing out loud to familiar songs on the radio.

Glimpses of the Salish sea, cruising through wooded corridors, it's like being in a dream. The air is real. It goes straight to your brain. The trees are gentle giants ushering transients along on their journey. I take a turn off into Fanny Bay and stand in the salty air, watching the active harbor for a few moments longer than planned. The island will do that to you. Time will shift. Breathing slows down. I take notice of that familiar feeling of just waking up. Stretching my arms out toward the sea, the weight of it all just thrown to the waves, then sinking down to the bottom where the oysters lay. Scanning the horizon. Carefree. Infinite.

My cell interrupts. A sound that doesn't belong in this moment.

I pull it from my coat pocket and glance at the text. Breathing a sigh of relief that it's Shaina. I call her number so I can hear her voice and know that this is real. I'm really here. On this side.

"Hey, sorry I got carried away with the drive and forgot to text you."

"No problem! I'm just glad you're coming! Make yourself comfortable when you get here, okay? The door's open. I have a client I need to get to, then I'll be back later this evening."

"Okay, I'm just in Fanny Bay now and I'll grab a coffee. I should be there in a couple of hours!"

"Don't finish all the wine without me!"

I laugh. My face feels tight and I realize what 'cracking a smile' really means. When was the last time I laughed? No doubt I will pour a glass as soon as I get into Shaina's kitchen. She makes her own blackberry wine and it's to die for. It's been a very long time since I've been able to enjoy that. Best paired with her company though.

A wave of guilt washes over me. I've denied myself this connection for so long. I'm angry with myself for that. I've been suffocating. That's how it felt to be in my skin, living my life on the other side of that water.

Enough.

I inhale another long breath of salty air that smells like freedom.

I get back into my car and drive. The road continues to flow along with my thoughts, and I begin to feel so clear headed, my mind surging with new topics and ideas. I've had that dreaded writer's block for so long I can't even recall what it feels like to have the energy to run with a story anymore. That feeling of brilliance when it first begins to weave together in my mind.

I wrote about Shaina once. When I was pregnant for Tally, her journey as a midwife and my own immersion in the very issue was the perfect backdrop for a story at that time. Midwives were caught in the throes of a modern day witch-hunt. The medical profession and government overreach dictated licensing for a practice older than all those decomposing white men in their legislative seats.

There's something about literary journalism that gets people's attention. The story drilled down to something a little more personal, easily finding a place to land in the minds of the common person. I remember writing with such rage. The new requirement for midwives to hold an undergrad degree, followed by a long examination, was just another barrier for women created by the grinding wheel of patriarchal bullshit.

Focus News picked up my piece and I was paid. I gave it to Shaina to help with her tuition. This brilliant woman and practitioner who already possessed the knowledge to guide a natural and ancient experience, would now have to endure almost four years of redundant education and debt, along with governing rules that did not quite belong to the essential nature of such a sacred practice.

We had my birth plan ready. It would mean being charged with illegal activity for her if caught, or if something went wrong. My plan was to stay at her place near the end of my pregnancy. Life has different plans for us sometimes.

6.

Arrival.

Entering Port McNeill after straight driving for over two hours was a welcome relief. My fuel gauge was showing an urgent need to pull in somewhere soon. I decided I could just park at Shaina's and fuel up on Sunday night when I made the trip back. A feeling of dread washed over me at the thought of having to go back and face Damien's anger over my surprise departure. Maybe Tally's too, depending on how much of his would affect her while I was gone.

If I get back on time like I said I would, then there shouldn't be an issue.

Glancing in the rearview, "Who are you kidding Cora?"

I turned down Shaina's street. Small ranchers lined the road, each with its own eclectic style. Hers was the most colorful. Brightly painted driftwood dotted the front landscape. Butterfly garden flowers were reaching and swaying along the walkway to her front porch. I parked the car in the driveway and slowly emerged, stretching my legs out onto the gravel driveway and whole heartedly welcomed the landing.

Her front door is unlocked, as expected. People don't need to lock their doors here.

I smell the hint of incense right away. It's permeated the place. Rich and soft. Comforting. The last time I saw her she gifted me a bundle of sandalwood and I tried to enjoy it at home. Damien threw it out. He said he didn't want his place smelling like some hippy commune.

I set my bag down and walked over to the hutch where she had a half burnt stick propped up in a large conch shell, a lighter beside it. I lit the stick, and then moved to the couch, immediately lying down in a long, full and glorious stretch. I don't remember falling asleep.

"Helloooo...Knock knock! Hello?!"

My eyes flew open. I'm horizontal, staring at a large fiddle-leaf fig plant. The sliding glass doors show it's dark outside already. For a moment I felt totally disoriented.

Then I realize I'm in Shaina's living room. But that's not her voice.

Suddenly very aware I'm alone in her house with a strange man who has just walked through the door.

An older, husky man is facing me in the middle of the living room. He's holding a stock pot and a warm smile. I sit up and feel relieved. A man holding a stock pot is here on friendly terms.

"Hi, sorry I didn't hear you at the door. Shaina's not here right now."

I started to get up, feeling a little light headed and decided to stay put.

"Oh man, my timing was bad! I disturbed your rest! Sorry if I startled you, I uh..."

He held up the stockpot to show me, as though I hadn't noticed yet.

"Oh, it's ok. Really. I think I've been out for awhile anyway." I stretch my arms over my head.

"Yeah, sorry I usually just let myself in. I actually know Shaina's not here, she told me she might have company though. I'm Gus."

Immediately I thought of the mouse from the Cinderella story. I smiled at him. This Gus here with me in the living room now was also stocky with a larger nose. I pictured whiskers and a small green hat. He seemed just as loveable. I smiled.

"Hi Gus. I'm Cora. An old friend of Shaina's."

"Yes, lovely. I've heard a lot about you."

He continues to stand in the middle of the room, holding the pot, staring back at me with a comforting smile.

"Can I take that for you?" I gestured toward the pot.

"Oh! Right...oh no no I've got it... that's okay it's quite full."

He moves into the kitchen and continues to chatter, "I made my famous mushroom chili. I hope it's okay with you, she invited me last week for dinner this evening and I was going to cancel if she wanted to because you were coming and it sounded like maybe you needed some time to... I mean just have some time to visit with her on your own but she insisted and then when she called and said she had a client she needed to go see, I thought I would just make dinner for the three of us!"

Well isn't this just the perfect life you've got going on here Shaina.

I chuckled a little to myself. Gus seemed very sweet. I could hear him rustling through the cupboards.

"Do you need any help?"

"I'm just going to whip up some cornbread!"

He continued to move items around in the large pantry, muttering loudly to himself, "I know she had a bag in here from last time we went shopping...aha!"

"Cora you're welcome to come in here and chat or whatever you feel up to. Have you heard from her at all this afternoon?"

I hadn't even thought to check. I grabbed my backpack and pulled out my phone. The battery was dead. I knew Shaina would have a charger, she had to have a cell phone for work. Of course I had forgotten to bring my charger. I probably forgot to bring a lot of things.

"My phone is dead actually, so I don't know."

"Oh, just use the landline in her bedroom. Give her a call and see if she's heading back to us yet."

Aha! These two are a thing! How else does he know she has a landline in her bedroom!

I'm smirking over my confirmed assumption.

Shaina never married but she had a son when she was twenty from a random hook up. She was so excited she would get to be the mother she never had.

He was stillborn.

I was with her and held her in her grief. She handled it so well. I could never have been that strong. Her father had also passed away a month after her precious baby was cremated. We spread their ashes together on the shoreline in Tofino, our forever sacred road trip destination.

Once she sold her dad's home, she decided to use the money and live her dream of seeing the world. She travelled for awhile after that. I remember feeling so lost without her during that time, but she kept in touch here and there. I worried about her, even though she was one of the most independent and determined women I've ever known.

She went from Alaska to New Zealand and chose to settle in Uganda on a work permit for six months. From her experience there working as an assistant to a group of midwives, she decided to start her own practice when she returned to Canada. She said it was healing and she knew now that the universe had given her the gift of childbirth to fulfill her calling. She returned to find herself passionate, fully immersed and on call for women all over the island. She did not face a single tragedy in any of her birthing experiences. The only tragedy was when she had to temporarily suspend her practice to spend years obtaining the licensing required by government rules. There were a few times she risked herself to help those women who refused what they considered a dangerous and low standard of care associated with obstetrical interference at birth. She didn't have the chance to risk it for me.

Damien made sure of that.

I picked up the phone and dialed her cell number. It went straight to her voice recording. I left a message, threatening to steal her mushroom-chili-making boyfriend if she didn't call back soon and let us know where she's at.

I took a moment to wash my face in the bathroom and run my fingers through my hair. As soon as I walked down the hall toward the kitchen, I felt pangs of hunger. The chili smelled delicious.

Gus was bent over the counter, carefully filling a loaf pan with thick yellow batter. He looked up at me and smiled.

"You know what the secret to a good cornbread is?"

I shook my head. My stomach was suddenly knotted with hunger.

"Jalapeno peppers! Gives it a good kick."

"Sounds yummy! I haven't eaten all day. I'm looking forward to this!"

"Oh well, you need to be my official test subject then! Here!" He poured a ladleful of steaming chili from the pot into a bowl for me.

"Grab a spoon and don't be too harsh a critic, this is my hobby of passion fused with a specific recipe my grandmother always used for chili. No meat. Loaded with my personal forage of mushrooms! Chanterelles, Oyster and a few Chicken of the Woods. Love that name! There were a few more worms than usual in the Oyster mushrooms this time but I'm sure I soaked them all out."

He grinned at me.

The spoonful of chili I now had in my mouth, held for a moment on those last words. I had to force myself to quickly swallow it. Then I gulped back a full glass of water.

"Too spicy? Sorry I always forget some people don't have the same tolerance. We have these TRPV1 receptors on our tongues and mine are apparently immune to spicy food!"

"What?"

"You know...how the chemical in spices activates those receptors? Some of us just have variations of tolerance because of the number of receptors we're born with. It's kind of fascinating right?

Okay, this Gus friend is a treat! Am I finally having an interesting conversation with another adult again?

I found myself pulled like a magnet to him.

"So what is that?"

"There's a chemical called capsaicin, usually found in chilies. It's one of my favourite spices actually. Have you ever tried chocolate with chili spice? It's beautiful. There's some theory that people who can tolerate very spicy foods have fewer of these receptors so less sensitivity to spicy dishes. So you may have a plethora of TRPV1. Not to fear! I am here to help you train those little receptors to welcome the burn! Your brain just thinks your mouth is on fire. That'll go away. Just eat at Chez Gus for a while."

He pops the loaf pan into the oven and snaps the tea towel off his shoulder. "Voila!'

I laugh and as I turn toward the sink to fill my glass again, Shaina walks into the kitchen with her arms open toward me, smiling.

"Now there's a face I haven't seen for a very long time!"

She wraps her arms around me and holds me in a warm hug. Her pashmina is soft on my chin.

She turns and gives the same greeting to Gus. He raises his eyebrows at me over her shoulder and smiles. Shaina turns and hugs me again, then sets herself down at the table. Gus starts setting napkins, spoons, a brick of butter, and some wine glasses. I offer to help. He pulls out a chair at the table. “Sit. Please.”

She inhaled the aroma.

“It smells amazing Gus! Thank-you so much for coming and bringing us dinner.”

He nods and bends forward slightly, the tea towel draped on his arm in formal fashion.

I’m searching her face for the outcome of her recent birthing event.

“How was your client?”

“It all went okay. She has some good support but I’ll stay on this one for a few months. She’s high risk for postpartum again... just some circumstances still at play there and she was pretty heavy into it for the first babe. This birth was a bit difficult. Little guy had a good sized head on him!”

Gus fills our glasses and we have a toast, clinking glasses together and enjoying a long sip of sweet wine.

“Oh God, I remember feeling low like that for so long after Tally was born. It’s awful.”

“I can tell you from my clinical viewpoint you didn’t actually have postpartum Cora, you were just married to an asshole.”

Shaina has a knack for saying it like it is in such a gentle way that you have to agree.

“Well I am still married to that asshole. I just don’t know how to take that next step and make that change.”

“I think you just did Cora.”

I shook my head, looking down into my wine glass.

"No. No I didn't. It's just a break for a couple of days. I just needed a break. I'm not taking Tally from him. She loves her dad. I know it's not good for her that we fight. But I can't support her on my own. And there's no way Damien is handing over paychecks. I'm sure he'd..."

"Cora stop. You don't have to figure it all out right now."

She put her warm hand on mine.

"Yeah. I know. Thanks."

Gus opened the oven door to check on the cornbread.

"Ah, just a couple more minutes to perfect this golden loaf of delectable delight and we will be ready! Vamos de fiesta!"

Shaina turned toward him, rhythmically clapping her hands. She got up and twirled in the middle of the kitchen, laughing.

He stepped toward her, arms raised and hands clapping, then they made quick steps together around the center of the kitchen.

I laugh and applaud their performance. Shaina smiles and gently pushes Gus toward the oven. "I think I'm distracting you from your catering job Gus."

"You two took dance lessons together? Cute."

Gus slapped his oven mitts on the counter before putting them on and opens the oven door.

"No no no my dear darling! Shaina signed up for beginner Flamenco lessons with me. I'm teaching at the arts center in town."

Gus a dance teacher? Where did this guy come from?

I made eye contact with her and we shared a smile. She knows what I'm thinking. She shrugged her shoulders.

"Good guys do still exist Cora. You should know. You had one, once upon a time."

I swallowed the rest of my wine.

Please don't bring that up. I know what I've lost.

I felt a tinge of annoyance, that old feeling of being judged crept up on me and I remembered why regular contact with her had faded. It was so damn easy for her to see what my options were, but they were not within my reach. Where she could be free and untied to walk through any threshold, I had passengers to consider on my journey.

I felt obligated to stay with Damien. Tally would not adapt well. For all his machoism and misogyny, he was just an injured bird. I knew what he had to contend with and endure throughout his childhood. His father abandoned him. His alcoholic mother hen-pecked him his entire life, and still he remained supportive. He took care of her when she decomposed into dementia.

Shaina disregards any arguments I have about the good side of Damien's character. She stands firm that none of that makes it okay for him to use me as his emotional punching bag. She just doesn't really know him. She never tried. I know him. It will get better between us. I have to believe that.

I just needed to get away and come here, to clear my head and see my life for what it is.

And to talk about what happened to me.

What really happened to me?

Gus is serving us the chili and cornbread. I was too hungry to continue to dwell on anything else in that moment.

I didn't have much to say during dinner. Gus and Shaina chatted back and forth about various local events. Gus asked me a few questions about my writing career.

What career?

We sipped through three bottles of wine before packing up the leftover chili. We said goodnight to Gus at the door, where he swayed a little holding his stock pot and slurred, "Buenas noches," when his cab pulled up.

7.

Strong Enough.

When I woke up in the morning, there was a note left on the kitchen table. Shaina was out on another call. I found some relief in this, as I welcomed the solitude. I knew at some point I would be pressed to talk about how I was going to change my life and stop making excuses. I wondered if that conversation was even worth staying for. I felt a wave of guilt and decided to check in with Damien. I wanted to know that Tally was okay.

I pulled my phone off the charger in Shaina's room.

Yeah just invite some more gasoline on that fire Cora. I'm sure he's dying to hear about how wonderful your visit is going.

Straight to voicemail. I didn't leave a message.

I decided that if there was something to worry about, he would call me and let me know.

He knows where I am. The question is, do I know where I'm going?

I filled my cup again. The strong coffee was a welcome start. Standing at the hutch in the living room I scanned the collection of literature, noting the titles on display.

Travel guides, a classic fairy-tale collection, origins of midwifery, a few unfamiliar fictional titles stacked together between pottery bowls filled with sage bundles and dried lavender. The Handmaid's Tale. Another title suddenly stood out.

Shame.

I'd be embarrassed to admit that I've never read any of Salman Rushdie's work. I pulled it from the shelf.

I felt that title. The word penetrated my brain.

I loosely flipped through the book, feeling the weight of its hard cover in my hands.

Shaina walked in the front door, setting a bag of groceries down on the coffee table.

"Hey! Good to see you're up! Did you sleep well?"

I slid *Shame* back in its place on the hutch.

"I did, thank-you. I slept really well actually."

"Probably because Gus used his special butter in the cornbread. Just a smidge!"

"Special butter? Oh! I thought it was the wine that knocked me out! He should probably tell people about ingredients like that!"

She shook her head and laughed.

“He wasn’t even thinking canna-butter would be an issue if you’re a friend of mine, I’m sure.”

“All I heard about was the worms. I don’t think I can ever eat mushrooms in anything again!” I faked a vomiting sound. “Just kidding. It was actually really good. He’s a nice guy.”

“Well, he’s a little different about things that’s for sure! But yeah, he’s great.”

“So, what’s this thing with Gus? Come on spill it!”

“Well you know, just having some fun with a friend. Nothing else. I want to hear about what’s going on in your life. We’ve got a lot to catch up on don’t we?”

I pick up the grocery bag and carry it into the kitchen. Shaina made a fresh pot of coffee.

“I’ll be heading back tomorrow night. I’ll catch the last ferry so I can make it to get Tally to school in the morning.”

She stands leaning against the counter, looking at me. Waiting for me to talk. Waiting to gather evidence.

“Damien knows where I am. I told him I just needed a break. Tally has been a handful. He’s working a lot. I’m feeling stuck and I haven’t been able to do any writing for awhile. Maybe I’m going through another episode. I don’t want anti-depressants again or I’ll have a really hard time getting back to my writing.”

I take a seat at the table.

“So he’s not going to be threatening my life this time for corrupting you? He’s over the whole Shaina is a shitty influence thing? You don’t think you actually need to leave an abusive situation?”

Shame on me.

"He's not hitting me or anything like that."

"Come on Cora! I can't even listen to you right now. He doesn't have to hit you to hurt you. I know you're smarter than this. I'm sorry, I know that's not being very supportive saying that, but I can't stand seeing you waste your life like this!"

This is not what I was expecting. Shaina doesn't usually react, she listens. She counsels me. I felt a surge of defensiveness.

Shame.

"Who says my life is a waste? I'm a mother Shaina. I have to be a mother first. I can't just pack up and leave forever. He would never let me take her and she wouldn't want to leave her dad either. I have to do what's best for her. You're not a mother. You don't get it."

I could see her clenching her mouth shut.

Damn.

"I'm so sorry. That was insensitive of me to say that. Of course you know what it's like to be a mother."

I don't make eye contact with her and quickly shift the conversation back to my domestic challenges.

"Look, it's just so complicated between us. You know we didn't have time to really get to know each other. I didn't get to have the fun friend thing with him first. Everything happened so fast with Tally and we're just making the best of it."

"So that's what you want to settle for?"

"I don't really see any other option Shaina."

"Living with a man who doesn't respect you, treats you like garbage, and who kills your creative mind is not an option. You're right Cora, you are a mother and with that comes the responsibility to teach your daughter what to expect from men. So what are you teaching her? That it's okay to just fade into the walls? Live for someone else? Jesus Cora, you only get to do this once! You're a brilliant writer. You can have your life too. You don't have to give it all away. Start standing up for yourself. Teach your daughter how to do that."

I gave a nervous laugh and rolled my eyes.

"Oh she knows how to do that, no worries there! I got called into the school the other day for concerns she's assaulting the boys."

She didn't take the bait on the conversation shift.

"You know you have options Cora. I've offered you a place here."

I look down at my hands, pressing my thumb into the palm until I could feel bone.

"I appreciate the offer. I've just got too much to take care of at home. I can't leave. Who would take care of my chickens? What does Tally do without me there?"

Shaina scoffs, "You're worried about the chickens. Cora, seriously?!"

I realize how ridiculous that sounds.

"Well, by the time I get home they're probably all gone anyway between Tally and the dog both killing them."

I swallowed hard, recalling the very cold and dismissive way she confessed to killing that rooster.

"What do mean Tally? Killing them?"

"Yeah, there was an incident with our rooster. But she said she had to kill it. He was attacking her."

"You tell me that she's fine, that you need to continue to stay for her sake. She's assaulting kids at school? Killing an animal? What part of any of that sounds healthy to you?"

"I don't know Shaina. I wasn't exactly raised in a house that had any semblance of normal either. My parents were never home. At least I know where my daughter is and who she's with!"

She takes a seat across the table and looks directly at me, her dark brown eyes intent on the message she's about to deliver.

"And if you continue to stay and show her it's okay to put up with that abuse and your unhappiness, then that is how she chooses her own partner some day. You know you're stronger than this. I know you're stronger than this."

This is not the conversation that I need right now. This is not why I'm here.

"I'm not like you Shaina. I'm not strong enough anymore. It's different for me. I don't want to fight. You know I don't."

"Then you will continue to die inside Cora. You will waste your gifts. Your spirit is lost right now because you've been lying to yourself for so long."

"I think a part of me was lost a long time ago."

I inhale sharply. Her gaze still penetrating mine. But I saw her eye twitch. I shift my gaze out the kitchen window.

"I've been remembering, Shaina. It's why I haven't been sleeping. I'm having nightmares. I had a serious blackout on one of my trail runs recently and I don't know if it's from the stress or something in my mind just keeps shutting down. I didn't come here to talk about Damien or what you think about my shitty life. I came to gain some clarity about what happened when we were in the woods that day after school, when those boys..."

Shaina closed her eyes, and took a deep breath. "We made a promise," she said in a quiet voice. "We wouldn't ever talk about it. It never happened."

"I know that. I know we did. I just feel so far away from it but at the same time, I'm starting to remember things. I have gaps in my memory of that day, like blackout stuff, and these episodes again too. I don't know why, but the last one I had was when I went for a run on the trail, and I don't know what triggered it, but I was holding this rock, like how me and Tally do this thing where we throw them into the ravine and....and I just passed out. Woke up with puke all over myself."

Shaina is tapping her coffee mug. The colour in her face was different. Pale.

"Maybe you should see your doctor."

"Yeah, I guess I should."

Her cell phone is ringing in her purse. She gets up to answer it.

"Okay well, off to bring a third into the world this week! There's some clam chowder in the bag, it's frozen but it'll thaw for supper. Just help yourself when you're hungry."

She moves quickly toward the door.

"Hey, if you want some company, Mary next door..." she motions to her left with her thumb out, as if she's catching a ride ..."loves a walking partner! I'll call you when I'm on my way home!"

A light drizzle had started. With the air almost constantly wet on the north end of the island, a walk was never postponed for weather. If Mary was any sort of character like Gus had been, then some fresh air with her this morning could be a welcome distraction and a good way to bide my time until Shaina returned.

And we'll have to return to our conversation. She must have some sense about it.

The real reason why I'm here.

I finished my coffee and borrowed a raincoat and gumboots from the entranceway closet, then made my way over to Mary's.

Calling on someone I've never met before stirs up a little anxiety in me. What if this person is still sleeping? Or doesn't want to take a walk with a stranger? I suddenly felt awkward. Also slightly annoyed again with Shaina, so easily leading me to do this.

I'd already knocked once, and no one has answered.

I decided I would just go back and get cozy with that Rushdie book.

As I was stepping off the front porch, I heard a knocking on the front window. I turned to look and a small elderly face was peering out from behind the white sheers, smiling and waving. She motions with her hand to come in.

As I stepped through the front door, she was already speaking.

"...and I was hoping you'd come by today! I was just saying to Aldus how wonderful it would be to go pick some salmonberries with our lovely neighbour."

"Oh hello Mary it's actually not Shaina, I'm a friend of hers, Cora. I hope it's okay, she told me you'd probably enjoy some company this morning? I'm just waiting for her to get back from a call so I thought I'd pop over and see if I could join you for a walk."

Mary was already shuffling toward me in her cable knit slippers. She smiles, pointing toward the kitchen.

"Just get that bucket from the bottom of the pantry would you?"

I slipped my gumboots off and went in.

There was a lit cigarette in the ashtray on the kitchen table, burning halfway through, with a long tube of ash hanging on.

"Is this your cigarette?"

Mary was bent over, her small frame pulling hard on a pair of boots. Her spine showing through her thin turtle neck sweater. She didn't hear me.

As no one else seemed to have heard my knock on the door, I assumed she was alone and stubbed out the cigarette.

"Help me with my coat would you please?"

Setting the small bucket down on the bench in the hallway, I pulled the arm of her coat up so she could slide into it. She stood at the front door as I quickly pulled on my gumboots and then opened the door for her. She turned in the doorway and motioned for me to get the bucket.

"Oh right, let me get that!"

She started down the steps and the front walkway with careful focus.

"Mary where do you pick salmonberries?"

She didn't respond.

Well, this won't be as lively a conversation as the one I had with Gus last night that's for sure!

I walked alongside this tiny woman, who maintained a slow, steady pace. We walked for quite some time, turning off from one neighbourhood street and then the next, coming to the end of a cul-de-sac, where the opening to a trail began.

Mary walked ahead. My pace had been slow and relaxed to match hers. It now quickened to keep up. We came to a wider trail lined with salmonberry bushes, some not quite ripe. I noticed the bear scat right away.

“Mary?” I used a loud voice this time, and clapped my hands out into the bush, being sure to make some noise in case there were any extra large berry pickers on the trail along with us.

She motioned for the bucket, taking it from my hand and putting her arm through the handle.

I leaned into her and spoke louder than I probably needed to.

“I think there’s been a bear here recently. We should leave!”

Mary gave a soft chuckle and started gently pulling the ripened thumbprint sized berries.

“She always leaves some for us.”

I circle around the width of the trail, trying to scan the dense forest and listen for any sound of approaching danger. I’d rather not wait around to find out.

Better to run through this place.

Mary speaks in a low voice. At first I can’t understand what she’s saying. Before I ask her to tell me again, I realize she’s speaking in her traditional language. I only know this because I recognize the words for bear and woman. Both words were part of the vocabulary I learned as a child, from the Elders who taught us some of the language in our elementary school.

I feel some level of comfort now, seeing that Mary had experience here, and was clearly in her element. I wished that I could decipher more of the language she continued to speak in low, soft tones. It turns to a melodic song.

I pull some berries and add them to her bucket. The heady aroma captures my entire being. The smell climbing through layers of my memory. It was both exquisite and terrifying all at once. We easily fill the bucket. Mary passes it to me. Without a word, she starts to walk back toward the entrance to the trail and homeward.

"My mom used to make a jam with these, if we didn't eat them all first! What are you doing with them Mary?"

She stops and looks up at me with a mischievous grin. "I just eat em all up!"

She steps back into her methodical shuffle. As we near her street, the rain starts to come down hard. We pull our hoods on and make our way to her front porch. She turns toward me and pushes her hood off of her eyes.

"You're a good berry picker Cora. You know that kind of place too."

"I did use to pick berries but not here. I lived in Port Hardy."

"That place where it happened. Where she saw you."

I feel Mary's eyes looking through me.

"I'm sorry, who saw me?"

I felt this might be one of those conversations where I'm stepping into someone else's altered reality. Near the end, Damien's mother had said some very strange things to me too.

Mary seems to be heading in that direction!

She pushed her finger gently into the middle of my forehead and chuckled. I did not move.

"You have a heavy mind. She will help you to see in that place. But first you'll find your soul mate again."

She winked at me and with that, motioned for her bucket of berries. She walked into the house, leaving me standing on her front porch, and softly closed the door.

8.

Remembering.

Shaina's Subaru pulled up just as I was stepping inside. I waited for her with the door open.

"False alarm Cora, I've got some time on this one. Whew! I need the break before another round!"

She looks me up and down, approving of my rain gear.

"You went for a walk?"

"Yes and met your darling little neighbor. She's interesting! She didn't have much to say on our walk but she did say something strange when I brought her home."

"Oh she's got some intuitive gifts that one. I just love her. She and her husband moved in last year. Poor lady just lost him a couple of months ago to lung cancer. He was really sweet too, terrible chain smoker though! I don't know how she could stand it. What did she say to you?"

"It was odd. She said something about someone seeing me, and I have to go to a place. Does she maybe have some dementia going on? There was a cigarette left burning in her kitchen."

"Oh shit. No she doesn't smoke. She lights that for him."

"For who? Her dead husband?"

"Yeah. I know it's concerning. She insists his spirit hasn't moved on yet. I check on her because I'm worried she's going to burn her house down."

We both nod at one another with an unspoken understanding of what that looks like.

Suddenly I'm feeling beyond exhausted.

"Hey Shaina, if it's okay with you I think I need to just have a quick little rest before we have lunch?"

"You read my mind, I need to do the same. Listen, you do whatever you need to here. I may be gone again when you wake up if I get that call, but if things aren't progressing, I'll be back quickly and we can dig into an evening of catching up! No more interruptions. Hopefully!"

I fall asleep on the couch to the sound of rain tapping on the front window.

No! No! Don't go in there! GET OUT!

Someone is yelling, I bolt upright. It's dark.

It was me. I was yelling in my sleep. A nightmare again.

"Shaina?"

No answer. I rub my face with both hands to try and become coherent and find my way to the kitchen. A note left on the table again.

How am I sleeping through her leaving the house? I'm never usually like this!

I decided I should check my phone. Maybe Damien had called me. Maybe he might actually want to check in on me now.

There's voicemail. It's Gus.

"Hi Cora! Shaina gave me your number and now you've got mine! If you want some company while she's out and about just give me a holler! I'm happy to come over and amaze you with some dance moves again!"

I close my phone and look out the sliding glass door to the back deck. Still raining.

No thanks Gus, no dancing queen here.

My thoughts go to Mary. I look at the clock. It's late. Too late to be knocking on an Elder's door.

I jumped, hearing the knock. I look out the window.

Mary!

I hurriedly answer the door.

"Hi! Everything okay?"

"Oh yes I'm just ready for our little talk now. I know you wanted to talk. I waited for you but you didn't come."

"Oh okay well... come in. Do you want me to make some tea or...?"

I think this lady is very confused!

"No I'd like some brandy."

I help her take off her raincoat.

"Oh! Um... I don't know if Shaina has any, let me see!"

"Yes she does, she keeps it above the stove for me."

Sure enough, there was a half-bottle of Bols apricot brandy.

Mary made her way to the kitchen table. She watched me pour a glass and put her hand up in a stop motion when it was almost full.

"I'm not supposed to drink very much. Thank-you, that'll do."

I sat down at the table across from her. She picked up her glass with both hands and slowly brought it to her lips. Her soft, brown hands were adorned with carved silver bands and on her left was a small tattoo. I hadn't noticed this about her when we were berry picking.

I waited for her to finish her long gulp of brandy and begin our conversation. She put her glass down, a satisfied smile lingering. She was looking into her glass. I waited.

Maybe she's forgotten the reason why she came over here?

I waited a few minutes more. She shifted slightly in her seat. Then she took another long sip.

"Your rings are beautiful."

Mary looked up at me from her glass. Her eyes opened a little wider and she put her glass down and laughed, holding her hands up in the air.

"There you are! I was waiting for you. My rings? Yes, they are. My brother was a carver. Rest his soul. There's one for you!"

"Oh! You don't have to give.... that's so lovely of you to offer but... I can't take that!"

Mary was pulling one of the silver bands over the gnarled knuckle on her right hand. She reaches across and places it on the table in front of me.

"It's a bear. It was meant for you. For your journey."

I reach for the ring and suddenly feel overwhelmed by her presence. Placing it in the palm of my hand, I felt the warmth still lingering from hers. It was a thick band, with intricate etching and that beautiful artistry I've known and loved for many years, but never awarded myself.

"Thank-you. It's beautiful."

I slip it onto my middle finger. It felt strong on my hand. Like armor.

"Now Cora. You have questions. We will do some talking. You should make some tea."

I sat looking at her for a moment.

Of course I had questions after her departing comment at the door today. I sensed that we would be enjoying each other's company for the rest of the night. I went to the stove and turned on the burner for the kettle, already full and waiting.

We went on until the edge of sunrise. Mary stood up and slowly moved around the table toward me, placing her hand on my shoulder and making a clucking sound. I sighed deeply. I felt a bit strange. Different. Something profound had changed in me.

She revealed knowledge. She pulled pieces of the story from me so easily, ushered from a place buried so deep I did not fully realize it was there. I had to remind myself this was real.

She made her way to the door. I followed.

"I'll walk with you. It's still dark outside."

Mary chuckled and turned to face me one last time.

"I can see through the dark. You rest. Then you'll go to that place with a clear mind."

I have to be getting home, how can I possibly do this thing she's convinced me to do?

But as this anxious thought began to slip around in my mind, it only flashed there for a moment. I now felt absolute conviction to continue on this path, to arrive at the end. To release the heavy stone that I was carrying inside of me. I curled up on the couch and closed my eyes for a moment, inhaling the warmth of this home.

My mind felt like a bright, full moon. It felt good to rest my eyes, to have the quiet, to hear my own breathing. It was steady now.

Full. Steady. Breath.

I organized my backpack and tidied up the kitchen, hoping that Shaina would arrive soon. I knew she wouldn't be able to make the trip with me but I had to tell her where I was headed and why.

She'll understand. Even though we don't speak of it, we knew this day would come.

When she came home, she saw me and she knew. She sighed and sat down on the couch, pulling the afghan over her body and up to her chin, looking at me with eyes of concern.

We talked about remembering that day in the forest. We had

carried this untouched thread, a safety line, between us for so long. Now it was vibrating and weaving an even stronger connection, vivid and crystal clear like the dew on a spider's web. Radial lines flowing outward from the deep corners of my mind, orb lines carefully constructed, holding pieces of that memory we finally spoke of now.

We both acknowledged the secret we had vowed to keep, but some details about how it all happened were foggy. She knew the terrible trauma she had seen unfold, but something was missing. She nodded slowly when I described the flashback of memories I'd been having recently, agreeing that it was time for me to connect to that place. To see the parts of the story that were missing. The pieces that were buried there. She knew that I wanted to face it alone. To be strong enough to do that.

There were tears for both of us. The hug goodbye was long.

"I'll let you know once I get there. I don't know what will happen, but I'll let you know. Whatever it is."

She nodded and hugged me again, tighter this time.

As I opened my driver's side door and threw my bag across into the passenger seat, I felt eyes on me. Mary was standing on her front porch. She smiled and then shouted, "Remember to pick the berries before you leave that place!"

I waved back at her. Sadness washed over me. I felt sure I would not see her again.

My fuel light was on. Somehow this didn't strike panic and anxiety in me like it normally would have. I planned to pull into the first gas station off the highway I could see. I was only under an hour from Port Hardy but somehow it felt like I was embarking on a long journey. It would be just enough time to mull over how I was going to execute this plan exactly. I had to remain convinced that I needed to go back to that place, to piece together what I could remember. I felt strongly that before I went there, I would have to see the old neighbourhood. I would take a walk on our beach and take it slow, before seeing myself for who I really am in that place again.

I pulled into a gas station, grabbed my credit card and went inside to pay for fuel. Perched behind the counter on a high stool was a larger lady looking down at a booklet in her lap. Her long, dark hair was draped over half her face. I placed my card on the counter.

"About thirty on the card please, pump three." I glanced around the store for snacks, suddenly feeling very hungry. She looked at me briefly, picked up my card and before swiping it, her eyebrows went up and she looked at me again. A broad smile spread across her face.

"Cora?"

Suddenly, I realized who was behind the counter.

"Denene!" She was heavier than when I last saw her.

'It's good to see you." She twitches her mouth into a half smile.

Hey, good to see you too."

"It's been a long time eh! What are you doin' back here? Comin' to see Will?"

I stood and stared at her for a moment.

"Yeah, it's been awhile! I'm just driving through to see the old neighbourhood. I'm not here long actually. I've got to get back soon. My daughter is home with her dad."

She looked down and tapped the card in her hand. I was unsure of what else to say.

"Oh I just thought that's why you're here. Of course, it's been a long time so I guess you haven't heard?"

I took a breath. I could see the sadness in her eyes.

"Um... is Will okay?"

Will was my first love. Denene's older brother. My forever happy place. What I remembered most about Will was how warm he always felt, inside and out. Even when we were swimming in the ocean, in the cold north island air. Fly fishing off the beach. Hiking the trails together. While he was my other best friend from elementary school, he was also my first crush, first boyfriend, and first heart break.

I made an annual excursion from the mainland to spend my summers working at the fishing resort there. We had reconnected during my initial summer back and comfortably slipped into a serious relationship. We were only eighteen, fresh out of high school in 1980. He had been hired as a line cook at the fishing resort. I had taken a position as a kitchen helper and dishwasher. We were excited to be spending the summer together. There was a crew of us, young and energetic, from all over the island and mainland, including two servers travelling together from Australia and a couple of housekeepers from Bella Coola. Will was the only local hire that first summer. We had the time of our lives. We spent long hours in the kitchen together and on other general tasks around the resort. The salary was decent, and of course we could use the lodge facilities. Even though Will could make it home after his shift, he often stayed with me. We spent our evenings and late into the night sharing deep conversations, fingers intertwined, lying on the bed together. Sharing the adventure, our bodies and our dreams. During my second summer there, I made my way into a serving position. Will enjoyed the kitchen and came back every season to work at the resort too. It helped make up for the time we had to spend apart, when I'd leave and go back to the mainland. He was able to make his way over to see me a few times, but it became more difficult as his family responsibilities grew back home. But we had our summers. Four good ones.

Even though the island felt like home, I just couldn't stay. There was something about being there too long that left me feeling nauseated. I always had to make a quick exit at the end of the summer work season.

The break-up was my doing when I decided to go to university and landed on a program in the Fraser Valley. I had opted then for work as a seasonal labourer for a landscaping company during the summer break, rather than making the trip and the expense to go all the way back up to the resort. The long-distance relationship we tried to maintain off and on for a few years after that wore thin.

After I finished my degree in creative writing, I worked full-time for a year with a house cleaning company to pay off my small student loan. We didn't see each other at all. Then we reconnected briefly again in 1988. One of us had to make a change so we could stay together and he wasn't leaving that place. He had great respect for his grandmother and was committed to taking care of her. He wanted me to stay. I couldn't really explain why that wasn't possible.

I shivered, suddenly feeling a chill.

"Will has cancer."

My stomach dropped.

Did Shaina know? Why didn't she tell me?

"Oh my God, I'm so sorry. No, I didn't know. Is he going to be okay?"

"It's okay, he hasn't been real public about it. He found out a couple weeks ago. I just assumed you were here because you might've heard. I should've called you myself I guess."

I couldn't find any good words. The past few years suddenly landed on me like bricks. I had made so many mistakes. I lost time with him. For what?

"Actually Denene, I had a different agenda for this trip. But now that I know, of course I'd like to see him while I'm here."

While he's still here.

"Can you give him my number, please?"

I picked up the pen on the side of the counter and jotted my number down on the inside cover of the booklet she had quickly pushed toward me. She rang up my fuel bill and smiled. She would give him my number. I wasn't sure if that made me feel sadness or relief. That pain had been put to rest some time ago. Was it a wound sealed so tight with scar tissue that it wouldn't open up and fester again?

One look at Will and I knew I would split open and not be able to complete this journey. I had to stay focused.

He would call. I knew that as soon as he heard from Denene I was in town and she had my number, he would call.

I was just ten minutes into the drive when my cell phone rang.

I sucked in my breath. One hand on the wheel, the other reaching for my phone. I flipped it open, not even looking to see who it was.

Aching to hear his voice.

Will. I'm so sorry. For everything. I should have stayed. I should have tried.

"Cora?"

Not Will. It was Damien. My stomach turned over. He didn't sound right.

"Hey. I'm taking a bit of a detour before I come home. Now before you get mad I just need to explain. I don't know how to tell you but..."

"Cora I'm not gonna be mad. I'm sorry things haven't been right. I've had some time to think."

What is this? What's happened?

"Is Tally okay?"

"Yeah she's fine. I'm keeping her home from school with me tomorrow. I'm not going into work this week. They cut my hours."

Ah. I get it. No paycheck means hey Cora, hey baby, let's dip into your inheritance fund.

My parents were excellent with financial planning. They saw windows of opportunity and invested money. They bought property. I was their only daughter. They made sure I was taken care of. They were still there for me, even though a truck went through my mom's windshield and my dad's heart shattered.

In case of emergency, break glass.

"Well okay, that's fine I guess. I'm actually heading up to Port Hardy instead of coming back right away. There's something I need to see. I'll have to just tell you about it when I get home."

"Yah sure. Hey, how was your time with Shaina?"

Oh man he's laying it on thick. Is he drunk?

"It was fine. She's busy so I didn't see her much. I'll touch base with you soon, alright?"

I could hear him just breathing on the other end.

"Damien?"

"I love you Cora. I really do. I don't show it and I know I need to do better. I mean it this time. I want you home."

"Damien are you alright?"

"Yeah I'm good. I'm better. I'll be better. I promise. Call me soon."

"Tell Tally she can call me at bedtime. Please?"

"Yeah, okay." He hung up.

I didn't say I love you back. I didn't even think to say it. Do I still love him? Did I ever?

I thought of Will. His big smile, his large, warm hands. His messy, tousled hair, like he always needed a haircut. His long hugs. The way he would put his hand on the small of my back when he pulled me in close for a kiss. He kissed me a lot. He was fresh air. He was my good place. He was there for me when I went dark. He knew why. He knew because I got drunk one night after a work party and the next morning, he said I told him something bad had happened to me on the trail when I was younger. We never hiked that way again after that and I wouldn't talk about it. He never pressured me to explain further.

I turned the AM radio on for a weather update.

No surprise there. High winds and rain expected overnight.

Then "Linger" by the Cranberries. That was the song. We were down by the water that evening. My last one there. He asked me, begged me, to stay. There was no reason not to at least try. I was resting my head on his chest, facing the fire. We were wrapped tightly together in a thick blanket from the back of his van. He hooked his leg over mine, leaned into my ear and softly sang the lyrics of the song playing over the small radio we had with us on the beach.

Suddenly my eyes blurred with tears and I took my foot off the gas. This road would not allow for mistakes. I pulled over.

Will was the last person I expected to hear having cancer. He was so strong. He was always running. Healthy. He didn't drink or smoke. He wanted to be a good mentor for the younger kids. There were a lot of kids who went sideways really bad in that place, mostly out of boredom. It wasn't something you would expect from kids in a place so beautiful and abundant. So vast. Too much maybe. You get swallowed up by it.

Then there was the healing for some, from generations of trauma, and how things had flared up even worse when there was finally talk of tearing down the residential school. It wouldn't matter. That place was haunting people whether it stood or not. Will was acutely aware of his relatives and the community members who needed him to be strong. They needed him to be there for them.

I just sat in my car on the side of the road and cried. I cried for all of it. I never should have left. I knew what I had lost and I knew what needed to be found. Or I would never be whole again.

9.

Going Back.

I hadn't even thought about where I would stay. It was only late afternoon, but I needed to be settled in safely somewhere before it was dark. Tomorrow I would go to the beach. The thought of that made me feel so incredibly happy. To be back in this place always brought initial feelings of joy and contentment. But once those dark feelings crept in, I always needed to leave.

That's not going to happen this time. I'm stronger now.

I decided to walk through my old neighbourhood before checking into the motel down by the airport. It wasn't something I'd ever allowed myself to do when I returned for summer work at the resort. I turned off the highway and entered the trailer park, slowly driving past where my parents had once set up their first little real estate investment. Theirs was the nicest lot in the neighbourhood, with a large trailer and extended deck. The corner lot with the large cedars. Now, just stumps.

The trailer looked terrible. They aren't built to last.

They burn fast too.

I pulled over, turned off the car, stepped out, and closed the door. The wind was starting to pick up. I pulled my hair away from my face so I could see. A semi truck roared by on the highway, the driver pulling the horn for two kids walking on the shoulder, pumping their arms in the air. I walked slowly to the center of the park, where the playground used to be. Where Shaina and I had spent a lot of time together at dusk, stalling to go home. It was just a dirt lot now. There were a few RVs parked. I looked up and down the road. Some places still showed a sense of pride, though most were dilapidated. A dog was incessantly barking from someone's backyard as I walked down to the laundromat at the end of the street.

The bulletin board posted outside the door had a few notices for rentals available, an ad for husky cross puppies, and a floral pastel couch for sale. I never really had to spend any time in there, as our trailer had an addition built on so there was a separate laundry room. But the kids all played around this building together sometimes. There were some good hiding places here. Once Shaina's little sister had hidden inside a dryer and scared the bejesus out of Mrs. Toper, the older lady who lived alone on the south side of the park with her one-eyed shepherd and a serious day drinking habit. After that, they put a code lock on the door. It wasn't until years later we understood the irony of her last name.

I started walking back toward my car. This all felt a little anticlimactic so far. The place looked the same, but it didn't. It was strangely quiet here too. Not like when we were young and there were always fifteen or more school aged kids running or biking around. I hadn't seen even one in the park yet.

Too quiet now.

And then there were the three that you never wanted to see. Those boys.

I stopped and looked across what was now a somewhat empty RV lot, toward the site where those boys used to live. The curtains had always been drawn shut. A rusted out grey truck in the driveway. I remembered their stepfather in coveralls, carrying a six pack into the trailer just before supper time. I once saw their mom passing him in the driveway, wearing her hospital scrubs as he yelled in her face, yanking her hair so hard she bent over before he let go and she got in the truck.

I remembered these details because I was a huge Harriet the Spy fan at the time and went around noting things about all the neighbours. Some inconspicuous and some not so much. I remember feeling sad for the lady who got her hair pulled. I always felt the undercurrent of something bad surrounding their place, like an aura of red-hot burning anger. There was just a smoldering black hole after the fire. Now a tidy little beige trailer stood, happily in its place.

Shaina and I were in her backyard just up the street, trying chin ups on her new swing set. Those three boys came through her yard like wild dogs, staring at us. The heavier one made a quick pivot and came over, smiling. He leans on the ladder to the slide. I didn't like his smile. His brothers stood back, putting their hands in their pockets, watching and listening. "'Hey girls," the heavier set boy said. I had never had the attention of an older boy before. It made me giggle a bit, uncomfortably.

But part of me liked it. He was a good looking boy. Shaina was quiet. "I'll show you how to do that." He jumped up on the bar, showing off a few chin ups. "Now you." He pointed at her. She was a little shorter than I was and she needed a leg up to reach the bar. That boy picked her up and as she reached for the bar, he slammed her small body down onto the ground, laughing.

That old familiar feeling started to rise from the pit of my stomach. I quickly began to walk back to my car. I started to half run, half walk across the street when a car horn cracked into my ears, along with the screeching of brakes. A woman leaned out of her driver's side window yelling, "You don't look?!!"

I put my hand up and shouted, "Sorry!" Catching my breath, I forced myself to slow down.

Stop it. You don't have to run. You're here. Deal with it. You're okay.

I took one last look around. I was more than ready to check into that motel now.

There was a liquor store attached to the Airport Motel and I stopped in there first to pick up a bottle of red wine. A sleep aid. I was probably tired enough without it, but it wouldn't hurt. I walked into the motel lobby, carrying my bag and my bottle, and waited for an attendant to show up at the front desk.

There's something about an older, outdated motel that always made me think of unfaithful married couples because of that year I spent as a young teen cleaning rooms. I saw couples who were trying to go through unnoticed, but were noticeably checking in without luggage. There was always a business guy with a receding hairline coming or going in a cheap suit too. These places smelled like old, stale cigarettes.

The attendant finally showed up. Yawning.

'Sorry, I was taking a quick nap in the back room. Courses are killing me right now."

"What are you taking?"

I was genuinely curious. I loved attending university. Even though I already had my English major completed, I still took the odd writing course now and then to keep myself tuned up.

Not that any of that is helping me these days.

"Just taking some business management courses in a hospitality program at the community college. Getting out of this shithole and running my own hotel somewhere someday."

"Well I'm looking for a room in this shithole for the night if you have one."

"Yeah, we aren't that busy so you're good. Seventy-eight for the night. Cash or credit?"

"Credit, thanks."

The attendant quickly checked me in, handed me a room key, and let me know there'd be a continental breakfast not worth having in the morning until about nine.

"Good to know. I'll let you get back to your nap. Best of luck with your courses."

He nodded and offered a smile.

I walked down the hall, counting room numbers until I reached mine. The carpets looked stained but the room was clean. I set my backpack on the chair by the bed and immediately looked for a drinking cup in the bathroom. Removing the paper cap from the cup and the screw top from my wine bottle, I poured a full glass.

Cheers to making it through step one here Cora.

I gave myself a little toast in the mirror. Being able to walk through that old neighbourhood, recall the first encounter with those boys, see it all again through these eyes now, was a start.

This is a good place though, despite what happened. I'm going to take the evil out of it. Put it to bed. Speaking of bed... that bed looks like a damn good idea right now.

But first I needed to call Shaina and let her know I made it. This far. And tell her about Will. Or ask her why she didn't tell me about Will. Surely she had known. She was all over this island and didn't miss much. I pulled my phone out and dialed her number. She picked up right away.

"Hey, I'm at the Airport Motel."

"Oh gross why would you pick that place? Couldn't you stay at the hotel with the pool in town? Or one of those cute little bed and breakfast places?"

"It's okay, I'm fine with it. And I'm a short drive to Storey's Beach. You know."

"Ah I wish I was with you so I could enjoy that too. Hopefully you get low tide."

"Yeah. Listen, I stopped at the gas station on my way through. You remember Will's sister?"

"You saw her then. She told you?"

"Yeah. When did you find out?"

I could hear her sigh deeply into the phone. I took a long sip of wine.

"About a week ago. When you called me and said you'd been thinking about me, that's why I said you've been on my mind too. I was waiting to hear more details about his prognosis before calling you about it. Did she say anything further? What stage he's at?"

"No. I didn't ask. I think I was in shock just seeing her, and then hearing about Will."

I could hear Gus in the background, shouting something inaudible.

"What did he say?"

"He says bring back a bucket of clams and he'll make you stew. He's making zucchini noodles tonight. I'm not excited."

I laughed. "Okay, well I'll let you go enjoy all that."

"Call me tomorrow, okay? You're okay right?"

"Yeah. I am okay. I think I should handle this just fine. I can do it."

I opened the heavy, beige curtains and sat on the end of the bed, looking out the window into the parking lot. I sat there in the quiet and finished that bottle of wine, watching the odd car drive past the motel. A seagull picked at a flattened chip bag on the road. Another seagull joined and they briefly squabbled over the garbage.

By the time I got out of the shower, it was getting dark. The seagulls had moved on. I fell heavily into that bed.

There was a faint knock on the door that pulled me from my sleep. No nightmares through the night. I felt amazing, although slightly dehydrated. I had the comforter pulled up to my chin, a nest of pillows around my head.

Why do they give you so many pillows?

A very loud and obnoxious crow was cawing outside the window. I waited for another knock which would have prompted enough reason to get out of bed and answer to who was invading my head. I didn't feel as annoyed about it as I usually would have. It was already bright outside and I figured it would be time to get going soon anyway. Then I remembered how bad the coffee was in places like this and hoped there was an alternative option close by.

There was no second knock.

I stretched under the covers and stared up at the ceiling for a minute, then threw the covers off and planted my feet, shuffling into the bathroom *like Mary.* I smiled a little, thinking of her. She was the reason I felt strong enough now to take this journey. The journey that was waiting for me and I hadn't even known it. I reached for the ring on my finger.

A bear is courage. I am a woman. I am a mother. I can do this.

A little red wine was left in the bottom of my glass and it turned my cool drink of water pink. I ran the hot water, soaked the single washcloth and wrung it out, stinging my hands with the heat. I held it on my face for a moment.

I was being slowly brought back to life since I had arrived on the island. And now, there was this feeling of strength and a deep urgency to face that terrible event we carried from the forest that day. I looked in the mirror.

There you are Cora. Welcome back.

I left the tank top on that I'd slept in and pulled on a light sweater and tights. I decided today was a good day to forget the bra. What was the point of it? This decision felt ceremonious. The path to complete freedom. I gathered up the linens into a grab sack in the middle of the bed and placed a five-dollar bill on the night stand. Slid on my runners, picked up my backpack and made my way out the door. I almost crushed the bouquet of flowers leaning up against it.

Oh geez, he is really laying it on thick!

The last time Damien sent me flowers was after our second date, after the first time we were together for the night at his place. Besides getting pregnant with Tally, it was the only time I got any token of love, and she was quite the prize token.

She didn't call me last night.

I scooped up the bouquet, pulled the small card from the centre and read it.

Want a good coffee? – Will

Of course he figured out where I was. There's no confidential guest code in a small town. He was probably friends with the motel attendant. I felt amused and smelled the flowers.

I made my way down to the lobby and approached the front desk. The attendant, who was actually wearing his name tag today, held a piece of paper out for me.

Will's number.

"Thanks Silas."

"Had I known you were such a special friend of his, I would have included this amazing tour guide, free of charge last night!"

He picked up a pamphlet off the side of the desk and showed it off, Vanna White style. I laughed.

"How is he? I heard about... what he has to go through."

Silas put the pamphlet aside, looking down at the counter and sighed deeply, "Yah well..."

"I'll call him soon. Thanks for this. Take care."

Silas gave me a warm smile.

The people here are good people. Most of them. It's not a place where you can be an asshole and survive easily. You need each other. It can be a harsh place. True North Island. There are just the right people to make it, and the tourism pours enough into the economy to make life comfortable but unspoiled. The wildness of it all cleanses you. Though some things outside of our control can taint that. But I see this place for what it really is. My home. It's where my soul lives.

I sat in my car, waiting for it to warm up. Mornings here are always crisp, even in late spring. I only saw the best of this place when coming back during the summer months for employment. Most months throughout the year are constantly wet and cold, but it keeps the rainforest alive and well. You get used to it though. Being at the gateway to the coast, with the flow of marine life and the backdrop of authentic, ancient wilderness, makes you feel so alive. You can run with the wolves. Everything is connected.

Working at the fishing lodge, we would sometimes have to put up with a regular group of Americans that would roll in, full of their greasy, macho shit and total ignorance of the real beauty of this place. They tipped well though, especially if they figured they'd get a hint of action from any of the girls running the lodge. They always got too drunk to follow through on those expectations. We made sure of it.

I pulled the piece of folded paper from Silas that I had tossed on the dash and saw Will's number hadn't changed. His house was near our old school and it was the same house he grew up in with his parents and grandmother. He lost his mom when we were in grade eight. She died of cancer. I don't remember what type it was, but I do know she seemed so normal to me, not sick like you see in the movies when people know that they're dying. His dad became very depressed and withdrawn after that. A year later he was out on his fishing boat alone. Will believed he must have accidentally gone overboard in the rough water. He was never found. Will was strong for his grandmother. She was strong enough for him though too. I had only been there for his mom's funeral. I will never forget the heat from the fire and the drumming. It went right through my soul.

I dialed the number on the paper. His land line. Hoping he'd be there.

It went to his answering machine. I almost hung up, but I stopped myself.

Don't be such a chicken shit. It's just Will.

His voice was so good to hear, even if it was just a recording.

"Hi, it's just me. I got your flowers thank-you, it's been a long time since.... Um, well I'm not here for long, I wasn't even planning on coming so it's kind of a surprise to me too, but I think it would be great to see you. Anyways, here's my number if you want to call me and maybe..." my babbling message is interrupted by the phone picking up.

"Cora!"

"Hey Will. It's so good to hear your voice."

And that's how I ended up sitting in his kitchen, still vibrating from the long, warm hug, with a great cup of coffee in my hand and looking at one of the most beautiful people I've ever known.

He told me about his diagnosis. He had not been feeling well for some time and because of the history in his family, he had some blood work done. Scans confirmed pancreatic cancer. Surgery was possible to remove the tumor found, but chemotherapy and radiation would have to come first in an attempt to shrink it and slow it down. He would be going in to start treatment next week.

"Will, why didn't you call me? Why didn't you tell me this was going on?"

"I just needed some time to figure things out for myself and I didn't want to burden you with it. I figured you'd know eventually. And now here you are."

He asked me about Tally, my writing, how I've been since my parents died. How happy he was to see me again.

He held my hand when I talked about the accident and my dad's heartbreak. I cried. I realized I never really got to grieve for them. We laughed about Tally and her incredibly strong will, her recent events, and my awkward meeting with the principal. He did not ask me about Damien.

But I had to ask him.

"Was there anyone else for you, after I left?"

It was almost too painful to ask.

Will looked at me. No one else except Shaina had eyes like that. Deep, dark brown, infinite. Seeing right into my soul.

I felt heat rising in my face. I pulled my hand away and played with the silver band on my finger, looking down.

“Don’t do that.” His voice was soft.

He continued to hold his hand out across the table. I placed my hand back in his, feeling the warmth radiate up my arms, through my chest. I closed my eyes.

‘Will I’m so sorry. I know it was a mistake. I should have stayed. I just didn’t know how to do that.”

“Cora, it’s okay. You can’t change the past. You have to move on. You wouldn’t have Tally if you didn’t leave. And you wanted to be there for your parents. And school. I get it.”

“I wish they had never left this place.”

Will squeezed my hand.

“What do you wish for now?”

I swallowed hard, pulled my hand away again and reached for my coffee. I drank the last of it, strong and bitter. I needed more. He was already getting up to pour me another.

“Well I’m here because I know I need to face my past. I think something broke open in me. I just snapped! Up and left in the middle of the night. I think I needed to run from being suffocated there. I can’t really explain it. I feel like I’m carrying too much all the time and I have to unload this thing that happened to me here. I need to let it go somehow.”

Will places the fresh, dark coffee in front of me and sits down again. He’s looking at me. I see his eyes scanning my face, my arms, concerned.

“Is he hurting you?”

I shake my head.

“No, no not like that. It’s not good, but it’s not all his fault either. He just... he just landed in front of me one day and I think I was rebounding from you and we moved into things too fast and then I got pregnant by accident. Not that she's a mistake, but I don't think it's what I really wanted."

Will looked out the window, then turned to me and said quietly, "Do you want to take a walk?"

I smiled, wiped my tears again, and nodded my head.

There was a light mist of rain. We pulled our hoods up and started heading down toward the beach. Exactly where I wanted to end up today. With this person. My person.

Will held my hand. We walked close together. Not another soul in sight, aside from the eagle flying low across the trees lining the beachfront ahead and the three crows perched on the overhead wire, watching us pass by.

Should I feel guilty for being here with him? Is this wrong? No. I didn't plan this. He's just being my friend. I need him right now.

Will smiled at me. In that moment, it felt like I had never left. It felt like the good times when we were together. So easy. Comfortable. Calm. Nothing like the sparks that you think are supposed to fly when people fall in love.

Is that even love?

No. This is. I know it now.

And I'm not afraid to be here anymore.

10.

Trail Ends.

Low tide. We step out of the tree line and onto the beach, feet sinking slightly into the wet, dark sand, rippled by the waves from the tide. Scattered empty clam shells and large bull kelp lay across the landscape. My eyes scanned for signs of whale traffic over the white caps in the distance.

I could hear Will breathe a deep sigh. He gently pulled my hand to his mouth and let a long kiss linger. Words fell from my lips with great sadness.

"I never should've left you."

Will put my hand down slowly and looked out over the ocean. He turned to look at me and smiled.

"I'm so glad you're here Cora. I wanted to see you again."

"Then why didn't you find my number and just call me?"

He shook his head.

"You have a family. And I didn't want you to feel like you had to see me or talk to me again just because I have cancer or because I might not have much time left. I only ever wanted you to come back if you wanted to. For yourself."

"I did come back here for myself. I've been remembering some things I must've been just blocking out for so long. It's why I could never stay here Will, even though I wanted to be with you. You have to know that."

Nodding, he put his arm around my shoulder.

"When I was at Shaina's something happened there with her neighbor, Mary. She saw things in me, things that happened to me. I don't know how to describe it. I just know that I have to go back to that place where it happened and face it. I came here to do that and I have to do it alone. Then I think I can move on and live my life."

I look up into his eyes.

"I want to live my life again Will and I want to start over with you. I realize that now. I just don't know what that will look like because I might lose you again and I don't know how I can live with that."

I'm searching his face for some sign of acknowledgment, to accept me back here despite the heartache I caused. He nods and meets my gaze.

"I'm not just waiting to die, Cora. It's how I'm going to live that matters. And I don't want you to be with me because you feel pity for me or think you owe me something. I loved you. I still love you. If you want to come back and be here with me, you have to be sure you're doing it for your own reasons. Not for mine."

"I want to be here because I still love you too."

A gust of salty wind whipped around us and the tall cedars lining the beach started to sway. The rain began to come down hard. Will pointed in the direction of home.

"Let's head back! I'll make us some lunch."

He scooped me up and carried me up to the tree line.

When we got in the door, our coats were so dripping wet, he had to grab a towel and mop up the floor in the entrance way. There was no raincoat that could win against the worst of the North Island weather.

We spent the afternoon making a soup with a few potatoes and an onion that were on the verge of drying up in the pantry. I found a pack of frozen moose burger, fried it up, and added it to the pot. We talked about his grandmother, her delicious soups always with bannock, her stories, her amazing life. Such a beautiful matriarch in the community. She had passed away last year. Some of her things were still in her room down at the end of the hall. I was sorry I wasn't there for him. I told him more about Mary, how she reminded me of his grandmother. Of my grandmother too. Sacred women. My mom loved being a grandmother with all her heart. Will reminded me that having Tally was meant to be. It was a beautiful gift for my mother to have that kind of love before she died.

The ease in which we moved around the kitchen together, coming close, laughing and touching, was so familiar. I didn't want to leave. The soup made me feel full, warm, and sleepy. But time was passing and I knew I had to continue on with the reason why I came here in the first place. The rain hadn't stopped. I had a few hours left before dusk.

"I think I should go. I want to make that hike into the trail before it's dark because... well you know."

I raised my eyebrows at him and we shared a silent understanding of the perils awaiting kids like us who venture into the forest after dark. His grandmother had been a storyteller and she loved to remind us of the Wild Woman who gathered wayward children to take them away and eat them up. While telling the story, she would reach out and pretend to grab Will, making smacking sounds with her lips, and then laugh showing her missing teeth.

"You could stay. The weather is terrible. What's one more day?"

I want to stay. Until it's your turn to leave me.

"The weather is always terrible."

We smiled at each other.

I left a message for Damien and Tally saying the weather had turned and I would need one more day to finish my trip here. Just one more day. I would let him assume I was still at the motel. I texted Shaina and let her know I was at Will's place and would head into the trail tomorrow. When I closed my phone, he slid his arms around my waist, burying his face in my neck.

The next morning, I found him sitting in the kitchen with coffee in hand, looking out the window. He didn't notice I had walked into the room until I put my hand on his shoulder. I was still wearing his t-shirt. We ended our little kitchen party last night with a long hug. Then he kissed me. If there had been drinks involved, we would have ended the evening differently, without inhibitions and feelings of responsibility. Things would have continued into the bedroom. I wanted to. I know he did too.

"It was nice to have your company here last night. Thanks for staying."

There was a strangeness in his voice. He sounded like a formal host.

"We're not saying good-bye, Will. This feels different. I'm going to carry on, but I'm going to come back this time. I want to come here and stay with you. I can do that. If you'll let me."

He shook his head.

"Denene is moving back in here next week. I don't need you to come and take care of me. I'll be fine."

That feeling started to creep into my stomach. Once you've lost someone you're not ready to lose, you know how it feels to carry the burden of grief. It doesn't dissipate over time, it compounds into something different, like heavy stones inside of you. Then you lose yourself under the weight of it.

"Well I won't be fine."

Will looked at me. He took my hand in his.

There you are. Stay with me Will. Please.

"You don't have to do this Cora. We aren't going to get to go back and live in the past. It won't be like it was. We know how this could end."

"This is home for me, Will. You are my home. I'm going to make it right."

"And what about your daughter? How does she fit into this?"

"I don't know yet. I'll figure it out. All that matters is that we'll be with each other again."

"Cora, that's what I've always wanted."

He pulled me in close and kissed me.

We agreed that I would call him as soon as I made it out of the trail and back to my car. As I drove away, he watched me, waving. Just like before. Only this time I knew I would be coming back to where I belong.

Smiling, I turned my focus on the road ahead.

Mary was right. I found my soul mate again.

The trail leading from the school along the south side of the forest heading back toward our neighbourhood wasn't far off. I tucked my car into the school parking lot and walked toward the trail from that end. The same route that Shaina and I had taken that day. I knew it would be about a twenty-minute hike into the area where we used to wander and pick berries or throw rocks into the ravine. Stalling long enough for our imagination to run wild and hear bears, cougars and who knows what else coming for us.

I would walk through this memory today.

Not run.

I can't run from this anymore.

My heart pounding now, as if I'd sprinted through the trail already. Plenty of daylight ahead quickly put me at ease. Shaina and Will both knew where I was in any event. No cougar sightings or warnings in the area today. I had my cell phone. Though the question was, did I have reception?

I checked my phone.

Of course not. But maybe it'll pick up again on the trail.

I took a deep breath as I walked in. One step and then another. One foot in front of the other. A few more steps and I started to easily inhale the forest. I felt it surrounding me like a soft cloak. I felt my shoulders relax. My mind stopped racing. My pace became rhythmic. My focus clear. Surrounded by vibrant life everywhere and yet I sensed I was the only being actively moving through it all in that moment. I walked on.

I had learned growing up in this place that you can sense a bear before you see it. You'll feel it's massive energy. They didn't usually bother anyone, and would turn into the forest before they would turn into the path of any humans going through their territory. They are wise animals. I had shared the landscape many times with a few bears, especially down by the river when the salmon were running. There was a respectful distance maintained by both parties. The difference being in the forest, is that respectful distance was trickier to keep, due to the space being filled by massive trees and a dense forest floor. And then there were the roots. Roots creeping in all directions. Gnarls humping out of the soil, reaching across to one another, creating a tripwire in the moment you might decide to slowly walk backwards from the mother bear rearing up to look at you so sternly.

Suddenly, I felt my focus break and sensed a charge in the air. There ahead of me on the trail now was the most massive black bear I'd ever seen in my life.

I stopped. I could hear my breath and feel my heart pounding through my entire core.

Easy. Steady. One foot behind the other. Slowly.

Okay bear. Okay bear. We are good. You go on. I'll go on. Don't look up.

Then she did. Eyes on me. Neither of us move.

This is what it feels like when time stands still, facing a formidable predator. As I stood frozen in this moment, I had the overwhelming sense that the bear was actually mirroring me. I lowered my gaze, bowing my head slightly, then glanced up to see any hint of direction from her to come. She had lowered her gaze and bowed her head too. I began walking slowly backwards again, careful not to misstep and careful to step a little higher, over the wave of roots.

And then I heard her release a deep huffing noise.

I let out a long exhale and squatted down in the middle of the trail with my head in my hands.

My heart was still pounding. It wouldn't stop. I felt like it was getting faster and louder.

I put myself into a fetal position and tried to take some breaths.

No air.

A tightness fell into my chest, my head started to pound harder, and a searing ache stabbed into my brain.

I felt so cold.

Everything went dark.

Long, sharp flames reach up like the devil's hands clawing at the air. Popping, cracking, and crashing sounds. We watched it burn. Others had gathered nearby. The fire burned so hot that the brown, billowing smoke funneled straight up into the evening sky. From where we were sitting across the park, we could see the small window on the side of the flaming trailer smash out. And then we heard the screaming. The same screaming we had heard in the forest. Only this time, they couldn't run.

The siren from the single fire truck in the distance, too late. The flames were shooting out of that window before they could.

I opened my eyes. My head lay heavy. A banana slug was gliding across the trail in front of my face.

Was it starting to get dark? How long did I black out for this time?

I slowly pushed myself up into a seated position. Forest floor debris stuck to my hands, small needles and soft soil. The bear was gone. I looked up into the canopy above and decided it wasn't actually getting dark yet. I realized then that I didn't have my watch on because I must have left it on the nightstand in Will's room. Would I have enough daylight left? I had to trust my instincts.

Hoping the bear had moved along enough for me to continue, I stood and took a moment to ground myself, feeling my feet planted firmly.

Here.

One foot in front of the other. Each step closer to the clearing by the ravine.

As I moved on through the trail, closing the distance between the life I've carried on with and what happened in this place, I felt like I was in a trance.

No fear, no anxious thoughts, no urge to run.

I could feel her now. She's here. The Wild Woman.

Her formidable spirit.

Her fierce mind.

I know her.

Closer now.

Closer.

The small clearing and the ravine were finally in front of me. Standing in the understory of this place, where the darkness could finally be laid to rest.

Entering now to see it all clearly. To see myself here on that day. To see it in the light.

To see it through her eyes.

Heaving slowly through the trees with desperate hunger, drawn to the girl lying on the forest floor. A larger boy there too, with his heavy weight on top of her. His hands around her neck. Her eyes pleading with me. The Wild Woman. Powerful. Ready.

The girl calls to me, opening her mouth in a silent scream.

The smaller girl held against a tree by the others. I smell their fear as they look at me, eyes wide. My focus is sharp now, drawn back to the girl on the forest floor.

I will devour that boy stealing her voice.

My hunger roars as my body lifts from the forest floor.

He did not see me coming.

I see what happened here now. I see it all. What happened to me lies here, in this place. I remember.

The boy whose weight crushed the air from my lungs, claws frantically at the ground around my head, dirt flying into the air as his body is sucked backwards away from mine. I scramble to my feet with sobbing breaths and look desperately for Shaina. She's pressed against a tree, eyes covered. A rush of cold air on my skin, soaked with sweat. My eyes burn.

The other boys, who had been holding Shaina back, are running. Screaming.

Their brother lay on the forest floor now as if he'd been thrown there, sprawled out on his stomach.

There's a large rock to my right. I pick it up. Moving in slow motion, I turn to see behind me.

She's there. Her wiry, long, black hair. Her mouth opening, ready to feast. Predatory.

I'm not afraid. She fills me with strength. She won't take us.

She will take what's left of him.

I heave the rock over my head and feel the skull of the boy crack again and again as he lies face down in the dirt. The boy who tried to kill me.

I step away. She descends upon him, and he's shrouded in her fury. She devours him before disappearing into the ravine.

I watched her do it.

Shaina and I held each other as we emerged from the trail, moving as one down to the ocean. I walk into the water and let the waves wash away the dirt and cool the abrasions. The water soothes over the fear that his hands had burned into my skin. We sit, huddled together. Something numb inside of us keeps us there for awhile. We watched the waves, and made a pact.

We weren't supposed to be that far into the forest. This never happened.

We walk along the beach and bypass the trail leading home, taking the highway shoulder even though we knew we weren't allowed to walk that route. But the semi trucks speeding past now feel much safer than any animal in the woods.

As we enter the trailer park, we smell the burning.

We stood in the playground lot, still numb, and watched the trailer burn. The boys' trailer lit up the evening sky. My parents were too distracted by the fire to be angry with me for being so late.

You're supposed to be home before dark or you might get eaten up!

They didn't even notice that my clothes were wet.

In the coming days, our parents talk amongst others in the trailer park. Mrs. Toper said she was sure she saw all three of the boys come home that evening.

"Must've been incinerated in that trailer," she would repeat for days.

She took in their mother, a small woman with a nervous smile who reminded me of the dog by the laundromat that was always chained up and who's owner kicked it sometimes.

The neighbourhood reached a consensus that it was a good thing the piece of shit drunk who was always smacking her around had left after the fire happened.

But terrible about the boys. Poor things.

It was probably his fault too, always locking them in their room together after she went to work. But the fire investigation only found two bodies. A missing child alert was issued for the other boy.

Shaina and I both lied to our parents. No, we didn't see that boy anywhere on the day of the fire.

About a week afterward, their mother was found standing in front of the charred lot. Screaming.

They admitted her for a mental breakdown to the same hospital she was working at that evening when her life burned to the ground.

Eventually, the fire investigator issued a final report in the local paper that read:

> "In response to the extensive fire damage on the scene of 8-777 North Rd. in Sage Park on June 4th, 1973, investigative findings determined the area of origin to be in the living room, then spread throughout the structure. The remains of two deceased occupants were located. The source of ignition was found to be inconclusive."

The other boy's body was never found.

I feel all the bones, the meat, the blood of memory alive and charging through my mind. Remembering it all so clearly now as I step over to the ravine and look down.

The ferns, mosses, and fungi untouched since that day I threw the large rock, marked with blood from that boy's skull, into the understory.

I picked a few rocks about the size of my hand that were scattered around the clearing and arranged them to create a landmark. A memorial to the burden that had been carried. Marking this place.

The place where I found the Wild Woman again.

11.

Moving On.

I almost didn't make it for the last sailing home. High winds had picked up and threatened to cancel the ferry. I wanted to take a quick detour and stop in for one more visit with Shaina, to talk to her and lay it all to rest for her too. It felt surreal. I wasn't even sure I'd be able to articulate it well, and it turned out I wouldn't have the chance to yet anyway. She was away on a call. But we both knew it wouldn't be long before we would see each other again. I would be back very soon. She wanted me to stay with her until I figured it all out. She would enjoy the company and I would be able to focus and write. Maybe pick up some part-time work at the local bookstore to get out into the world again. It would be a short trip from her place to spend time with Will while he went through treatment. I would stay with her until I could make a decision on the best arrangement for my life with him. He was prepared to go through a difficult time and we could only hope for the best. I wanted to be there for him. He deserved that. We would live for whatever we had left together.

I just needed to get back to Damien and Tally and follow though with the plan. Thankfully, the ferry stayed on schedule, although I felt seasick all the way.

I welcomed the quiet ride alone on the highway to think about how I would approach this next chapter with Damien. It might be difficult. It seemed the last time we spoke he was having an epiphany about our life together. I worried about what I was going to do with Tally.

A new start would be good for her. She could still see her dad on weekends.

Or it didn't have to be that way.

I could be the weekends.

Regardless of how it was going to work out, it would be whichever way Damien and Tally wanted it to be. That was the path of least resistance. There would be no more conflict. Tally had only ever known the undercurrent of resentment and animosity. She was born of it. Now she needed to be set free too.

When I arrived home, it was almost midnight. I tucked the blanket up around Tally's shoulders and kissed the top of her head. She rolled over onto her side and mumbled something in her sleep. Damien was watching the news in the living room. I sat beside him on the couch. He didn't look at me and we didn't speak for a moment. He motioned at the television.

"Big wind storm on the island eh?"

"Mostly just a lot of rain. The ferry home was a bit rough though."

He nodded and turned to look at me. I forced myself to look at him and start talking.

"I know you said you love me, but this isn't what love is supposed to be. What we have is obligation."

He looked down. I waited a moment for him to respond, then he looked up at me. I could see he wasn't going to be able to speak. I could see the tears coming.

They must be tears of relief.

"Damien, I think we will be okay if we can just work together but separated, and sort out how to best take care of Tally."

Damien rubbed both of his hands on his face and nodded his head. For all the years we've been miserable together, he didn't abandon us like some men would have. He could have easily walked. Sometimes I wished he had, but I know in my heart that wouldn't have been right for Tally. She loved him.

"Cora... when?"

I had thought this over on my way back. The long drive allowed for a solid plan to be sorted out in my mind. I was feeling a bit shocked at the ease in which this conversation was unfolding and how he seemed to already know what was coming. Maybe he had some time to think on it too since our phone conversation.

I had expected the usual tension, the hard argument, the blame for things not working out. *Stupid bitch.*

But there was none of that. We were both quietly accepting our place in this moment.

"Cora, listen. I want Tally to stay here with me. She shouldn't have to leave her school or this place. It's better that way."

He already knew that I would be the one to go.

I nodded in agreement. We sat together in silence and watched the rest of the news before parting ways. He would sleep on the couch. I touched his shoulder before I walked out.

"Thank-you, Damien."

There was nothing more to be said.

Over breakfast, Tally took the news exactly the way I thought she would. Shrugging her shoulders, continuing to focus on the business of putting a thick layer of peanut-butter on her toast, and offering no response.

"I'll take you to school until the end of the week and then I'll be leaving to stay with Shaina. But Dad will meet me at the ferry on the weekends with you and you'll get to come and visit."

Tally looked at me and narrowed her eyes.

"When you're gone, do I have to take care of the chickens?"

I looked sideways at Damien.

"Well, don't you want to? I can't take them with me. They're still ours. But if you don't want them anymore..."

"Only if I can sell the eggs and keep the money."

"Sure, you got it."

The only other negotiation I had to make before I would be discharged of my full-time position was to promise she wouldn't have to share a bed with me at Shaina's. She didn't want to "deal with the crazy stuff" I did in the middle of the night. I woke her up too many times with my nightmares. I was pretty sure that wasn't going to be an issue anymore, but I agreed anyway.

I spent the rest of the week packing what I needed. I wasn't interested in worrying about splitting up material things. Shaina had everything we needed anyway, and I wanted to make it a light move. There had been enough heaviness.

Damien stayed out of my way. He had a few work shifts to spend his days with, and when he was home in the evening, we were okay. I didn't mention anything about Will. I kept that whole situation all to myself. It wouldn't be a necessary conversation anyway.

It was already a story planted and waiting to grow in my next life.

On the morning of my last day before making the move to return to the island, it dawned on me that I hadn't taken Mary's advice to stop and pick the salmonberries on the trail, in that place.

Later that afternoon, Shaina called to tell me Mary had passed away peacefully in her sleep. She had found her when she went next door to invite her for a walk, to fill their buckets.

For Mary, I would make a point of going again, to the place where the understory held our secret. Shaina agreed that she would come too. The berries would be so much sweeter then.

I would write about it.

Excerpt from the memoir, "Returning to My Roots,"
in the feminist literary journal publication,
Storykeepers, Spring edition 2003:

For every woman who has ever journeyed to find themselves, we emerge in a place like the understory; those layers within a forest between the soil and the sky. It may be difficult to reach the light in this place. What lies here can either give us strength or devour us.

Trauma interrupts this journey of growth, as it can be so easily buried in those layers. Some of us are given strength enough to pick it up and keep growing toward the light. Others find trauma too heavy, and are pulled back down to become entangled with gnarled roots in the dark.

Mother trees shelter the young ones, the vulnerable saplings in the forest. They offer resiliency from the harsh elements, from high winds and hard rain. Their lives interdependent, roots interconnected. Growth does not happen without that connection. We can take lessons from this place.

We must continue to reach for each other, to grow from our stories, to come out of the dark and reach for the light. We need the power of feminine strength behind us to do it.

Our sisters, our mothers, our grandmothers.

Sacred protectors.

The Wild Woman in all of us.

CORA BUCHANAN

Acknowledgements

I humbly acknowledge that this story was written on the traditional, ancestral, unceded, and shared lands of the Stó:lō people, of Sq'éwlets, Leq'á:mel, Sema:th, Matheqwí and Qwó:ltl'el First Nations; peoples of this land since time immemorial.

Great appreciation is extended to those who offered consultation to ensure respect for Indigenous culture. Edits were made to remove traditional names and language from the fictional character's memory and experience.

I have been so fortunate to learn from some very talented teachers and authors. Trevor Carolan introduced me to literary journalism and inspired me to write "Frog Legs in the Rearview Mirror" for *The Cascade*. Miriam Nichols encouraged me to dig deep and explore what's possible. Andrea MacPherson taught me the value of patience and perspective. Her creative writing course brought this story to life.

A special thanks to Lee Maracle, the teacher who lit the fire in me, and who taught me the power of story. Her spirit lives on in my own teaching. Huy ch q'u (Thank-you).

I have fond memories of my parents cheering me on as a writer. They helped me publish my first piece of writing as a child in *Owl* magazine and what a thrill that was! They always told me to keep writing, and to publish my work.

Without the talented contributions of Michelle Fairbanks of Fresh Design, publishing this piece would not have been possible. I am grateful to have had her professional services and her patience!

Manufactured by Amazon.ca
Bolton, ON

36058528R00083